Short Stories

of A

Long Life

Alvis Brister

authorHOUSE®

AuthorHouse™
1663 Liberty Drive
Bloomington, IN 47403
www.authorhouse.com
Phone: 1 (800) 839-8640

Published by AuthorHouse 05/23/2020

ISBN: 978-1-7283-6304-2 (sc)
ISBN: 978-1-7283-6303-5 (e)

Contents

Foreword

SHORT STORIES OF A LONG LIFE

By Alvis B. Brister, Jr.

The contents of this book are in 4 parts, divided according to the major divisions of my life.

One - is the announcement of my birth and developing years as I progress toward adulthood.

Two - Our Married life from our first meeting and through our lifetime.

Three - My military service.

Four - Teaching years

Five - Texas Rehabilitation Commission Highlights

Six - Retirement and Ranching activities

Short Stories - Fiction

The Appendix

    A. Abbreviations used in the TRC years

    B. Copy of the letter announcing my birth

    C. Brief Brister and Vogt Family History

My birth was technically in the last year of the Great Depression, 1934. However, we were not magically rich or well off immediately. We did fare better than some because Dad was a school teacher with a regular salary, although not a big salary, but with that, and living in the country most of the time with gardens and chickens and a milk cow, we did manage to have plenty to eat. Clothing was more utilitarian instead of dress up, but Mom kept us clean.

The purpose of this book is to tell my children, Grandchildren, Great Grandchildren, and other readers, of the pre electronic era how boys lived and played before the electronic age came about with cell phones, computers, and games. We used our imagination to create games, toys, and unique methods to entertain ourselves. This will also tell how some of the adventures and games placed us in various degrees of danger, but we didn't know, or realize, how dangerous they were. We were saved from danger by our Guardian Angels. I stress Angels, because I am sure we went through several with our daring stunts. These stunts are well illustrated in the first part of this book, and vividly describe the things that "normal" or "sane" boys shouldn't do. I also hope this writing is amusing and will provide some laughs and enjoyment to the readers.

This also is a brief introduction to my family to help identify my standing within the family, and to introduce my brothers and sisters. There were seven children in our family. La Vona Aileen, Ghyatt Vaughn (Bill), Me, Alvis Benjamin, Jr., Mary Louise, Robert Price, Eva Geraldine, and Sandra Jean. In the early years there was just La Vona, Bill, me, Mary Lou, and Bob (Robert Price). We did not keep our given names, but had nick names like Pete, Bill, Junior, Mary got to keep her name, Bob, Jeri, and Sandy. Jeri and Sandy were involved in later years.

Our Dad, Alvis B. Brister, Sr., was born in Stamford, Texas, was moved to Oklahoma by his parents some years later, living near Atoka, Oklahoma. He finished High School, and enrolled at Oklahoma A&M in Engineering. He met his future wife, Flora Tidwell, who lived at Matoy, a small community East of Atoka.

After they married, Dad became a school teacher in order to support his new wife. As you read the different stories, etc., you will notice that we lived in many parts of Oklahoma. The reason being that Oklahoma did not have a State salary schedule for teachers, and Dad, through his many contacts, would be told of a school district that paid a higher salary, so we would move. We lived in the Northern, Southern, Western, Eastern, and middle of the State over the years. In spite of some shortcomings, there were good benefits to moving around. We did not make too many new friends because of moving, but we did develop strong family ties. Bill and I were not just brothers, but best friends also. Of course, La Vona being the oldest, was also very bossy. We didn't care much in our early years, but she became a bit of a bother as we got older. In all fairness, she was a great help to Mom, and she wasn't really mean to us. Some of our wildest times came about during the time Dad was in the Army during WW ll. You will read about these times later.

ABBJr.

Chapter One

My First 21 Years

My story begins with the announcement of my birth in a letter Dad wrote, which started:

"Hello Grandpas, Grandmas, Aunts, and Uncles,
Just a line to let you know that I have just arrived, as hale and hearty a 91/2 pound boy that you ever saw. I am somewhat mad at this time, will be better later. My hair is black. I would love to see you soon.
Lovingly, Alvis B. Brister, Jr."

Dad continues. P.S. he came unexpectedly at 12:36 a.m., February 15, 1934. Flora got along just fine, compared to the previous times. She wondered if you would still come about Sunday. Well, Flora and "he" are both asleep and we are thinking of taking a nap. La Vona said to tell Grandma she could sleep with her. Well, good night. ABB

The "we" he referred to was La Vona. The letter was written about 2:00 a.m. on the 15th, so Dad was ready for a nap.

This was the beginning of a life filled with the expected and unexpected events which have led to the present day. My life story proves that there are Guardian Angels, and that people can survive with the Grace and blessings of God. I have no memories of the first couple of years, only what was told to me by Mom. The first two years we lived in a rural area of Payne County Oklahoma, near Stillwater. They had community names, usually where a school or church was, but you couldn't call them towns.

Apparently, I was an inquisitive child from the beginning. One morning when I was two, Mom had gathered the eggs and put them on the kitchen table. She went about doing other things in the kitchen. Having been given the wonderful ability to walk, I went to the table and put the eggs on the floor. Then I went in search of a hammer so that I could find out what was inside the eggs. I quickly found the hammer and proceeded to check out the contents of the eggs. Mom said she heard some noise, but didn't bother to check until about the sixth "bam". She remembered I was in the kitchen and decided I was the cause of the "noise". She quickly separated me from the hammer and eggs. Being only two, I didn't have to clean up the mess, but I did discover the contents of eggs.

In 1938, Dad moved us to Butler, Oklahoma which is in the Western part of the state because he had gotten a teaching job that paid more salary. The move was in early spring and Mom was pregnant with Bob. Butler is located on a flat plain, subject to wind, hot summers, and blowing snow during the winter. Uncle Albert Tidwell was on leave from the Marines and came to visit and see Robert Price (Bob) for the first time. He was really a striking figure in his uniform. It was in Butler that I first remember my guardian angels watching over me. Our house was located fairly close to an arroyo, and since Bill and I had nothing better to do, we decided to cut some steps in the bank so that we could climb out of it. We used a double bitted ax, one that had a cutting blade on both sides of the head. Being rather young and not too strong, I had some difficulty in lifting the ax over my head to get a good cut into the bank. On the first attempt to lift the ax, I managed to get the axe over my head, but the edge of the ax blade slid along the back of my head and opened a rather decent cut. Naturally there was a lot of blood because scalp wounds always bleed extensively.

Mom got the bleeding stopped, and bandaged the wound. While the cut was healing, we had one of the good snow storms known on the plains, and we were fortunate to have a really tall and wide snow drift close to the house. This was excellent for Bill and I as we were able to tunnel into the snow drift, make a cave, walk on top of the drift and I was even able to lose a shoe which was not recovered until the snow melted.

My next head wound was a result of a broken jar. Mom collected the pieces and gave them to me to take out to the trash barrel. I dutifully dropped the small pieces into the barrel, but being me, I had to throw the big piece with the sharp point into the barrel. As my arm went over my head to throw the glass into the barrel, the sharp point opened the nice scar I had made with the ax. Once more the bleeding, bandage, and time to heal.

Grand Pa Brister was diagnosed with Cancer of the Bladder, so when school ended we packed up and moved back to Payne County to be close to Grandpa. Dad had been hired to teach in the school in the Fairview Community, which was close to Grandpa.

I started to school in the first grade when I was five years old in a one room school at Fairview. No idea why it was so named, but it was a group of houses and farms that required a school and a teacher. Also, it was very close to Grandpa Brister. Grandpa was very ill with cancer and Dad had moved close to him to help care for him and his farm. Having an older brother and sister who were in school already and who enjoyed "teaching", I had learned to read and do some simple Arithmetic so my Dad, who was the teacher in the one room school, allowed me to start. I was so excited on the first day of school that I got up early, got my Big Chief tablet and pencil, and took off out the door at a dead run. Mother called me back and asked me if I had forgotten something. I said, "No, I don't think so." Mother held up my pants. I looked down and saw that I had put on my shirt and shorts, but not my pants. After getting completely dressed, I then took off for school. I don't think there was any happier kid than me at that time. I loved to read (I still do), and I absorbed everything I could so that I could learn how to read big books. I guess my penchant for reading was the reason I didn't do too well in Arithmetic. I learned enough math to get by, but I would still rather read any day.

The school, as I mentioned, was a one room school. Dad taught grades one through eight. He would start with the first graders and let us read and what not, and the other grades would be working on assignments. Then he would go to the next grade and get them started. I never thought much about it then, but now I marvel how well he maintained control. I do remember that he let some of the Eighth graders tutor the younger students.

Easter was the time when everyone bought new "Easter Clothes" to wear Easter Sunday. The new clothes were a symbol of the resurrection of Spring as well as the Resurrection of Jesus. Anyway, I had a new suit: white short pants and a nice navy blue jacket. The following day, I begged, and cajoled, and pleaded, and promised anything if Mother would let me wear the jacket to school to show it off. After a while I finally wore her down and she let me wear the jacket with the understanding that I had better keep it clean. Of course I promised I would.

Our school had outdoor toilets, one for boys and one for girls. The outhouse had two holes but had not yet put covers over the holes. I had to use the facility, so I took off my jacket and put it on the seat beside me. After finishing my business, I reached for my jacket and somehow it fell into the pit. I was heartbroken and then scared out of my wits, because I knew what Mother would say. I thought it would be to my advantage to get the jacket out, and so I went out to find a stick long enough to reach into the pit and maybe get the jacket out. I tried and tried, but all I seemed to do was push it deeper into the contents of the pit. Finally, I gave up. It was warm enough that I didn't need the jacket so I was able to go the rest of the day without it.

When I got home that afternoon, Mother asked me where my jacket was. I said that I guess I forgot it at school. She told me that I better go back and get it before Dad came home and locked the school doors. I went back and told Dad that I had left my jacket there, but someone must have taken it because it wasn't there anymore. Dad, being a lot smarter than I thought and a lot more observant, quietly pointed out that he seemed to notice I had the jacket when

I was excused to go to the toilet, but I didn't have it when I returned. Finally, I broke down and told him about the jacket falling into the pit, and how I had tried so hard to get it out, and that I was sorry it had fallen in. Since we have a tendency to block unpleasant memories, I can't remember what happened when I got home and the whole story was told to Mom. I am sure it wasn't too drastic as I am still here today.

There were a lot of things that happened that year while we lived in Fairview just outside of Stillwater, Oklahoma. It was there that my brother Bill and I learned some new words from Dad. Dad was fixing up the chicken pen one Saturday, and Bill and I were very interested in the work he was doing. We watched very closely because we figured we might want to build something someday, and we needed to learn as much as we could. (Bill is two years older than me, so I was five and he was seven). Dad was hammering away when he missed the nail and hit his thumb. He grabbed his thumb and sort of danced around, saying some "new words" sort of under his breath but loud enough for us to hear them. We actually thought this was funny, and we were really enjoying the performance. We started to giggle, and then laugh, and that was too much for Dad. He, as they say now, lost his cool and verbally and physically pointed out to us that hitting a thumb with a hammer was not really funny, and his gyrations and mutterings were not meant to be a stage performance. We got the point, but we still thought it was funny.

We had a small trailer that Dad pulled behind the car and it became a play thing for Bill and I. The tongue of the trailer was on the ground, so we would climb on the trailer, run to the back, which was in the air, and it would drop to the ground, raising the tongue and making a good bump when it hit the ground. It was fun and we would spend a lot of time running back and forth and getting our thrills out of the trailer falling and bumping the ground. Our dog, Mitchell, decided to get in on the fun, and he came running to the trailer just as the tongue was falling. It hit him a glancing blow on his back and side, and we thought we had killed him. He yelped and sort of dragged himself to the woods around the house. He was gone for a couple of days and we were sure he was dead, but he came back and seemed to have recovered from the injury. He avoided the trailer after that, and we were more watchful when we were playing.

I want to tell about Mitchell now, because he was involved in our lives for many years. Mitchell was given to us by our Grandpa Brister. He was black and white, and I guess he was part Border Collie or cow dog. Anyway, he was extremely intelligent and very protective of the family. He also survived a lot of things that should have killed or maimed him. The first incident was when he was a puppy. We had him on top of the hay wagon which was loaded with hay, and was about ten feet high. Mitchell was romping around and got too close to the side of the hay and slid off and hit the ground pretty hard. He yelped and cried and we thought he was seriously hurt, but thankfully he was not. He was about a year old when the trailer incident happened.

Another time, Mother and I were walking across the pasture with Mitchell, headed to the woods to pick polk sallat, a natural plant that was like spinach. Our bull, who was not known for his sweet disposition, came charging after us. We tried to outrun him, but we really had no chance of doing so, and Mitchell knew that. He ran to the bull, got in front of him, and tried to head him away from us. The bull was persistent in wanting to get to us, so Mitchell jumped and grabbed the bull by the nose, pulled his head to the side, and caused the bull to fall over. The bull's nose is very sensitive, and when Mitchell pulled on it, the bull tried to turn far enough to ease the pain, and this caused him to fall. This allowed us time to get over the fence and safely away from the bull. The bull tended to give Mitchell a wide berth after that.

Living so close to Grandpa, and Dad going there every day to help out with some of the chores, Bill and I would go with Dad and spend time with Grandpa.

He had a knife that was very sharp which he used to cut a piece of chewing tobacco from the plug. I asked if I could borrow the knife to cut a stick and Grandpa said" you will cut yourself". I begged him and told him I would be extra careful. He relented and let me have the knife. After a while I came back in the house and handed him the knife. I had my left hand in my pocket, Grandpa looked at me and said, "let me see which finger you cut". I said none, he told me to show him my hand. The game was over.

Bill and I always wondered what made the tobacco Grandpa kept chewing so good. We decided to check it out. We took a plug of tobacco and went out behind the barn to chew some. Huge mistake. We didn't realize you had to spit the juice out. Instead we swallowed it and promptly paid the price. I don't remember ever again in my life of being as sick as I was that time. We gave up chewing tobacco for good. Since there was no television or play grounds around, we made our own devices for entertainment. Grandma always had a good garden and when she picked cucumbers, she would discard the large and tough ones. These discards became "live stock for Bill and me. We took used match sticks and pushed them in the ground, tied string to one and then go around all the sticks for our fields. We used the cucumbers for our cows and horses by pushing match sticks in for the legs and attach a piece of cumber to the front to make a head, thus we had live stock for our farm. Our vehicles were made from wooden cheese boxes, that had held two- pound blocks of cheese. When we made roads, we went modern by using ashes from the wood stove that looked like (sort of) concrete. Imagination is a wonderful thing

During 1940, Grandpa Brister was very ill with cancer of the bladder. To help out, Dad moved the family to Grandpa's so that he could help with the farm work. We had been living in a rented house about a mile from Grandpa. This was where Mitchell really showed his intelligence. We (I use the term "we" a lot), but it was Dad who mostly trained him to herd the cows. Grandpa had about eight cows that were milked and the milk was sold to a cooperative. We would tell Mitchell to get the milk cows, and he would go to the pasture, separate the milk cows from the rest of the herd, and bring them into the barn. He saved a lot of time and steps for us. We moved around fairly often because Dad, as a school teacher, moved to the places that paid more salary. Mitchell moved with us, of course, from the Northeastern part of Oklahoma (Stillwater and the near vicinity) to the far Eastern part of Oklahoma (Cameron, which is near the border of Arkansas). Mitchell was about 12 years old when he died. He was a real outside dog. One time there was a rabies scare in Ripley, and we wanted Mitchell in the house so that he wouldn't get bitten by another dog or animal. We got him inside after quite a struggle, but he took out the screen door getting back out as soon as we turned him loose in the house. It was in the early 1940's when a song came out called "A Boy and His Dog". It was about a dog called Shep and told of some of the activities of Shep and the Boy. It told how Shep nearly gave his life several times to save the Boy. It was a sad song, and it made me cry when I heard it because of Mitchell and all that he had done for us. Dogs are by far the most loyal and generous animals God created. They ask for nothing but food and love. They will even make their own shelter if you don't provide one for them, and will give their lives for yours.

While we lived in Cameron, there was a scare of an escaped criminal in the area, and Dad had to be away from home that night. Mom told Mitchell to not let anyone in the yard unless she said it was o.k. One of our neighbors who Mitchell knew, and had come to the house several times, tried to come into the yard.

Mitchell would not let her until she called for Mom and she told him it was alright. He let the neighbor in the yard then. What a dog! I still get sentimental about him although it has been many years since he died, and we have had other dogs when I was still at home and after Mary and I married. Back to my story.

My third year in school was in Ripley. Dad accepted an offer to teach in another district which paid more money. In order to be closer, we moved to the town of Ripley. This was still in the vicinity of Stillwater. Grandpa Brister had died and Grandma had moved to Porum, a town in Eastern Oklahoma near McAlister where her sister, Grace lived, so that she would be close to family. Ripley was small, but had an Elementary,

Jr. High, and High School. My third-grade teacher was young, blonde, and beautiful, and I fell in love with her. Her name was Miss MacDonald. My fourth-grade teacher was older, and her name was Mrs. Seaman. She was at least 30 years old.

The small schools always had an Easter Egg hunt and picnic on Good Friday. We didn't get out of school like they do now, but we would take a picnic lunch to school, and we would go to some farmer's pasture or to a park, and the teachers would hide the eggs, and we would hunt for them. There were prizes for finding the most eggs, and a special egg which was good for a big prize. Unfortunately, I never won any of the prizes.

We were living in Ripley when the Japanese bombed Pearl Harbor and WWII started. This was the beginning of the most patriotic era in American History. WWI generated patriotism, but not to the degree of WWII. Never before had so many people been willing to sacrifice their own comforts for the sake of the soldiers who were giving their lives and bodies to protect the American People. We had rationing for sugar, gasoline, rubber tires, red meat, coffee. Automobiles, although not rationed, were not built because of the need for steel and other metals to build tanks, trucks, ships, jeeps, and airplanes and other machines of war. Many cars spent a lot of time on blocks because tires could not be bought. All cars had a sticker on their windshields which told how many gallons of gas you could buy each month. Each family was issued so many tokens to buy red meat, sugar, and coffee. Scrap metal drives were always being held. and people were encouraged to take all scrap metal in for "our servicemen". A lot of time was spent in scraping the foil off gum wrappers and cigarette packages. Later, they did not use foil at all. Because of the need for green paint, one cigarette company had a slogan showing their part in the War. "Lucky green goes to war". Lucky Strike cigarettes used to come in a green package, but they went to white packaging so that they wouldn't use the green dyes. Other slogans were: "Loose Lips Sink Ships," "Walls Have Ears," "Your Scrap can Sink Japs," and many others. There was a great effort to finance the war by selling War Bonds. You could buy a bond for $18.75, which would be worth $25.00 in several years. In addition, you could buy savings stamps for 10¢ until you saved enough to buy a bond. They would also have bond drives with famous movie stars and entertainers making appearances to urge people to buy bonds. We even had these drives in small towns. We would have a Box Supper auction. The ladies would prepare a meal for two people, put it into a box, wrap it prettily, and put it on a table so that, supposedly, no one knew who prepared the box. People had a way of finding out which box their "sweetheart" had made, and would bid on this box. The auction was a lot of fun because there was a lot of involvement in the community, socializing, gossiping, and a chance to eat out. Most of the meals had chicken because chicken was not rationed. A lot of money was raised at these functions. Patriotic songs were written, and many servicemen who had performed heroic acts were honored as heroes. Audie Murphy even went into movies as a result of his heroic actions in WWII. Eddie Rickenbacker was honored as a hero because he was not only an "Ace Pilot", but had survived being shot down and floating on a raft for many days in the Pacific Ocean. *The Sullivan Brothers* was the hottest movie because it was based on the lives of five brothers who all volunteered to go to war and were assigned to the same ship which, unfortunately, was sunk in one of the major naval battles.

My personal heroes were my Father and Uncle, Albert Tidwell, United States Marine Corps. Albert had joined the Marines when he was sixteen and had been around the World at least once before the WWII started. He fought the Japanese in Guadalcanal, Tarawa, Tinian, and several other Islands, and was about to be landed at Iwo Jima when the generals of the Second Marine Division decided that they had had enough, and pulled them back and sent in another Division. Albert was fortunate in that he did not receive any wounds, and in fact, received a battle field promotion from Master Sergeant to Second Lieutenant as a result of all the officers of his company being killed or wounded and not able to command the company. The closest he came to harm was a bullet going through his pant leg, but not touching his skin. He had a lot of medals and eventually retired after serving a tour in Korea in 1951 and 1952. My Dad, even though he never went overseas, was a hero because he left a wife and six kids when he was called up.

In Ripley, they had a fun event for the children. They took several hundred pennies and one dime, and scattered them along a dirt street and then sort of plowed them into the ground. The kids were turned loose to find as many pennies as they could, and again there was a prize for the one who found the most pennies and a special prize for the finder of the dime. A War Bond was the prize for the dime, but I don't remember the prize for finding the most. I do remember that we got to keep the pennies we found.

A roller-skating rink was built in Ripley, and this is where I learned to skate. It was great fun and occupied a lot of my spare time.

Ripley is the place that Bill and I were most active in doing dumb things, and that caused some of my guardian angles to retire. The following activities took place in 1940, 1941, and 1942. Not all at one time however.

Like most boys, tree climbing was a must for us. We lived in a house on top of a hill that was across from a wooded area. There were some magnificent trees there, so we had to climb them. One big tree had a large branch that had fallen next to the tree trunk. I used this as a step up to help me reach the first branch. Bill had already climbed pretty high, so I was in a hurry to catch up with him. I reached for the next branch but it was dead and promptly broke and I fell across the large limb at the trunk of the tree. It knocked the breath out of me, and I couldn't get any air into my lungs. I was rolling around, bending over, standing up, and nothing worked. I still had no air. I guess I was trying to scream but I don't know if I was successful. Bill evidently saw me and came down from the tree faster than Tarzan, pounded me on the back and bent me over. Anyway, something worked because I began to breathe again. My angel prevented me from breaking my back. Did that stop me? No. A few weeks later, I was visiting a friend and we began to climb a tree in his yard. About a third of the way up, I somehow missed a limb and went falling through the tree limbs. Being an oak tree, it had a lot of branches and they were scratchy. Down I came and landed on my back, again, in a farm wagon but it didn't knock the breath out of me, and when I looked over, I saw a pitchfork with the prongs up and me about two inches from the prongs. My guardian angel was on the job. As I said, the tree branches were scratchy and I had multiple scratch marks on my arms and face. My buddy knew what to do. We went to the house and he got a bottle of vanilla and put some on the scratches. Many years ago, vanilla had a high alcohol content, so it burned like fire as he put it on me, but it kept away any infection, and it smelled really nice. Mom commented on the nice smell when I got home.

Ripley was not large enough to have a public swimming pool, so we had to go to the Cimarron River to cool off. We had found a nice deep hole under the railroad bridge and we would dive from the bridge into the pool. One day we had a lot of rain so we had to wait a day or two for the river to go down, and sort of clear up. At last it was good enough to go swimming in again, so off we went to the bridge and swimming hole. Since our ages ranged from seven to nine years, we weren't smart enough to check the depth of the hole. We never thought about it filling in. Up on the bridge I go, and dive off into the hole, which was not a hole anymore. The rain and river movement had filled the hole until it was only 2 feet deep. When I hit the water, my hands and arms took most of the shock, but there was still enough force to push my head and neck down into my shoulders. I was stunned and didn't move for a few minutes. Eventually I was able to move around. No more diving there. We decided that it was too dangerous and went looking for another place to swim.

While we were walking along the river, we spotted some wet areas and we knew we had located some quicksand. Now we could have some real adventures. We went out to the quicksand, walked in and then we fell backwards so that we were floating on top of the quicksand. By moving our feet, we could push our way to solid ground and climb out. Our parents did not know about this or we would have been chained up at home. The other fun thing was riding whirlpools. Fortunately, the river wasn't too deep and the whirlpools didn't go very deep. When we waded out into the whirlpool, we sort of messed up the circular motion so we had to wait a bit for it to get moving again. Round and round we go, until we forced our way out...

After the river began to dry up from lack of rain, we had to invent some other way to beat the boredom. We went back to the rail road bridge, and decided that this would be a good place to play. We tried various ways to walk across the bridge. On the rails, on the ties only, alternating from rail to tie in a staggered way. One day, while in the middle of the bridge, we heard the train coming. There was not enough time to get to the other side so we did the only thing we could. We dropped between the bridge and the tracks, holding on to the ties while the train went rattling across. Thankfully it wasn't one of the long trains. We had one more fun thing with the railroad. Ripley was one of the places the railroad had as a junction place. They had a small house where they stored some equipment and a hand car. We discovered that the railroad did not lock the house, and that the hand car was easy to push out onto the tracks. Once out, two of us would get on either side of the handle and push it up and down and move the hand car along the tracks. We were careful to not get very far away from the house, and not take chances of a train coming along. We were never caught and didn't damage the hand car.

Not all of my Ripley adventures were so exciting, at least to me. Ripley was the place where, I think, all of us caught Measles, Mumps, and maybe Chickenpox. We couldn't be considerate on Mom and get them all at the same time. We had to go one at a time, even Dad had the Mumps. After I had the Mumps and had to stay home, I got restless and since I had no fever, no swelling, and no problems, I decided to go check out the school. When I got to the school, it was recess and all the children were out playing. My Fourth Grade teacher was out and she saw me coming. She freaked out and so did the other teachers. They thought that I would start an epidemic of Mumps. I was told, since I seemed to be over them, to have the doctor sign a note that I was okay to go to school, but I had better go home now. Mom took me to the doctor and he said I was over the mumps. I went to school the next day.

During the summer, Dad had a job in Stillwater delivering Coca Cola to stores restaurants, etc. Bill went along to help since he was a big ten years old. One very warm day, I decided to fix a cold drink for him when they got home. Bill was partial to grape sodas, so I found an indelible pencil and prepared him a cold bottle of "grape" soda. The indelible pencil had a "lead", that wrote like a pen if the "lead" was wet, and could not be erased. When dissolved, it looked like grape soda. I put some lead in the bottle, filled it with water, and put it in the refrigerator. When Bill and Dad got home, I gave the drink to Bill. He was really appreciative. Until he took the first sip. I might have gotten away with it if I hadn't laughed, but I did and Bill took after me. I ran outside and he cornered me by the side of the house. He drew back his fist to slug me, but I ducked and he hit the side of the house, really banging his fist. He started crying/ yelling and threatening me, but he hurt too much to chase me. By the time he quit hurting, he was pretty well over his "mad" and left me alone.

When we lived in the big yellow house, we had a dirt road by the side and we used this for a "Shinny" field. Shinny is a kind of field hockey game, except all equipment is home made. The sticks are limbs we could find that had a curved section that loosely resembled a hockey stick. The puck was a condensed milk can that had been beaten into a sort of round shape. It was very solid and could really travel.

This one unfortunate day, I was the goalie. Here comes the "puck" at a gazillion miles per hour. I tried to stop it, but it deflected just enough to hit me in the mouth. I still have the chipped front tooth. We called it shinny because the shins did take quite a beating in a hard- played game.

We moved from Ripley to Cameron, Oklahoma, in the far Eastern part- almost on the Arkansas State line. I was in the fifth grade, and it was here that I won my first and last boxing match. I was champion of the fifth grade after I bloodied the nose of another fellow student during the boxing finals. I retired as champion. It was still war time, and we were limited in what we could do for entertainment. We mostly did things where we could walk to them. Even if we weren't rationed in gasoline, we were rationed in money, so we had to do things that were inexpensive. I became a fan of basketball, and Bill and I would spend a lot of time shooting baskets and playing one-on-one with each other. Dad was always looking for work we could do to add money to help with expenses. He heard that the large spinach companies, across the border In Arkansas were hiring workers to harvest the spinach for canning. LaVona was hired to work in the canning factory while Bill and I were given a basket and a knife. We had to crawl on our knees, or stoop over to harvest the spinach for canning. We would cut the spinach off at ground level, put it in the basket, and when full, take it to the truck and receive a dime for the basket., get another basket and repeat the process.

We made a couple of dollars each day.

Cameron is where Dad was drafted into the Army. Mother moved to Matoy as a stop-gap measure until we could find another place in Durant, Oklahoma. We moved to Durant in late summer of 1943 and moved into an apartment there. What a life. It was one of near poverty and desperation, although I don't remember that part. Mom had only the government allotment from Dad to live on and provide food, clothing, shelter, and some luxuries like candy or a movie once in a great while. How she managed to do this and keep her sanity, I will never know. Durant was where Bill and I, without the firm hand of Dad, came really close to getting into trouble. The things we did to get money for movies, etc., were not always the best way. Soda pop bottles all had two cents deposit on them so when we wanted extra money, we walked the streets and alleys to find the bottles, turn them in and get the two cents for each bottle. We learned that milk bottles were worth five cents, so we would look for them also. Not many milk bottles were thrown away, so we had very few to turn in until we found a "cow nest" that had quite a lot of bottles. We would only take three or four at a time because we wanted to have a source to replenish our funds. Alas, one day our supply of bottles dried up. We had to locate more bottles. Well, here is the sticky part, we found that one grocery store put the empty bottles at the back of the store in the alley. We would take some bottles, wash them out, and take them to another store to get the deposit. As was evident later, this was stealing. Twenty-five cents was good for one day of pleasure. Movie tickets were a dime, popcorn and a coke were a nickel apiece, and an ice cream cone after the movie was a nickel. The movie was an all day affair. Usually a double feature, like two cowboy movies, a cartoon, a newsreel, and coming attractions lasted for three or so hours, and we would sometimes sit through them twice. Occasionally I would get to carry a box full of popcorn bags up and down the aisles and sell them to the customers who didn't want to go out of the theater to get popcorn. This was another way to see the movies free. We also hired out to clean the theaters in the mornings before the theater opened. There were three theaters in Durant.

We continued "honest work" in the summer. Mom's Uncle Felix, had a small nursery and he would hire Bill and I to help him dig holes to plant shrubs, etc. He also let us borrow his reel type push lawn mower. We would go up and down streets looking for lawns to mow. For some reason, Bill would not go knock on a door and ask for work, so he let me do it. I didn't mind because Bill would do most of the work. Unfortunately, Uncle Felix was becoming an alcoholic. At this time, Oklahoma was a "dry" state, no alcohol over 2.5 per-cent beer could be legally sold in the State. Bootlegging was a flourishing business. When a person wanted a bottle, he would contact the local bootlegger and buy a bottle, or call a taxi company and turn in the order and it would be delivered to him. For show, just prior to an election for Sheriff, the incumbent would stage a "raid" on one or two bootleggers, and make a big production of smashing bottles and dumping the contents down the sewer. The bootleggers were happy to supply some bottles for show since this guaranteed them immunity from being shut down. This is leading to the time Bill and I got into the business. We would walk the railroad tracks and alleys looking for empty whiskey bottles. Every bottle always had a little bit left in it, so we would pour this into one bottle. We would continue doing this until we filled the bottle. We would take it to Uncle Felix and he would give us a couple of dollars for the bottle. I think our bottle was a VERY special blend of whiskey.

Finally, I found a real job, rather Mother found it for me. She went to work in the Bakery shop, and they also needed someone to clean out the cake pans for the next batch of cakes. This was a good job for me, but I had to get a Social Security Card, which I did. After a time, the owner decided I was worthy of dipping the doughnuts into the glaze. This was very easy, put a dozen doughnuts on a slender stick, dip them into the pot of melted sugar glaze and hang them on a rack to crystalize. I was happy to do that, and when the owner told me I could eat what I wanted, I thought I had really reached paradise. However, after six or so doughnuts, I couldn't eat any more, and smelling the sweet glaze was almost overpowering. I realized the owner was smart because I would not be eating one every now and then and interrupting the glazing procedure.

April, 1945, was the month that World War Two ended. Great celebrations were held and the soldiers began to come home, Dad included. He was discharged in 1945. After adjusting to civilian life, Dad made contact with various schools, and was hired to teach Math in Bokchito, about fifteen miles from Durant. We prepared to move, tires were available so we got the car off the blocks, loaded up and moved to Bokchito. Sandra was born at Bokchito in 1946. Since La Vona had graduated high school and moved to Dallas, Texas to work, and Bill would not think of taking care of a baby, I was the designated babysitter for Sandra to help Mom. Sandra was not a problem to care for. I will say that her first distinct word was "damn". My friend Frank had bright red hair and Sandy wanted to touch it or pull it, but Frank kept moving his head and not let her grab it. This is when she said damn. Sandy was bottle fed and I made up her formula each day.

Dad was also the basketball coach which was great for Bill and I. Bill and I both were on the team.

Bokchito is where we lived when I joined the National Guard unit in Durant. Bill had gone to the weekly meeting of the unit, got some enlistment papers and had Dad sign them so he could join. After a couple of meetings, I went with Bill to one of the meetings. The Unit was trying to get up to strength so the Sargent asked if I wanted to join. I told him I was only thirteen, but he said if Dad would sign the papers, I could join. I took the papers home, and as the War had ended, Dad felt it was safe enough to let me join. He signed the papers and I became a member of the 45th Division of the Oklahoma National Guard. I was assigned the Browning Automatic Rifle (BAR), A great weapon, but heavy. I loved the weapon, and easy to shoot since the recoil was forward, and did not "kick". I placed second in high score for shooting the BAR but it was hard work so when the Unit needed a cook, I volunteered and was sent to San Antonio, Fort Sam Houston to train as a cook in 1948. I was so good that in 1949, I was sent back to Mess Sergeant School, and trained as a Mess Sergeant. The Mess Sargent was in charge of ordering supplies, preparing menus, and supervising the cooks and K.P.s for the Unit. I had a lot of fun in San Antonio because I got a Class A Pass that was stamped "Adult", which meant I could go into places that sold drinks and had floor shows. I visited many of the tourist attractions, but enjoyed Playland Park, Breckenridge Park and the Zoo most. While I was at Fort Sam Houston, Bill joined the Air Force and was sent to Lackland Air Force

Base for basic training. I went to visit him at Lackland, wearing my uniform with my Sargent stripes. Basic trainees were required to salute any officer or Non-Commission officer, so I received a lot of salutes. We had a good time. The Korean Conflict started about this time, and because I was only sixteen, I was discharged from the Guard.

Dad had gotten a position as Principal of the school in Manitou, Oklahoma, and had moved there while I was in San Antonio. It was a small town near Frederick, Oklahoma which was close to the Texas border, not too far from Borger, Texas. I began to "star" as a basketball player in Manitou, and we won several tournaments. I got my first flat top haircut there, had my first serious romance, and my first car wreck. I can't tell you the name of my first love because I forgot it. So much for "never ending love". The car accident came as the aftermath of my sixteenth birthday. Mom had really gone all out for this party. She let me invite a few close friends and she fixed a great dinner, steaks and all the trimmings. Everyone was having a good time, but one of the girls had to go home. The only person with a car did not want to leave the fun to take her home, so he asked me to take her. The car was a pretty, red Ford convertible. I took her home and as I was coming back, the car hit a patch of loose gravel and gently tipped over on its side. I was not even shaken by the accident. I crawled out of the window, and walked down the road to a farm house and asked the farmer if he would get his tractor and pull the car upright. He said okay and went to get his tractor.

Meanwhile, there was some concern because I should have returned to the party so Dad and the owner of the car came looking for me. They arrived the same time as the farmer with his tractor. The farmer hooked a chain to the underside of the car and pulled it upright. There was very little damage to the car. The convertible top had a small tear on the side. I was not hurt and the owner drove the car home.

From Manitou, we moved to a small town named Dibble, a consolidated school district and not much else. Dibble is located between Chickasha, and Purcell, Oklahoma. Dad rented a place in the country that had a couple of barns and about 40 acres of land. We had running water, because Mother was always telling me, "run out to the well and get a bucket of water". I played baseball and basketball at Dibble, and was a "star" forward in basketball and was a pitcher and alternated at second base in baseball. I was also President of the Future Farmers of America (FFA) Chapter, and I raised show pigs, (Berkshires) to show at the County, and State Fairs. When showing the pigs at the State Fair, we had to sleep in the barns where we kept our animals. It was cold, so I slept next to my pig. He was washed and clean, and the straw was clean and I slept comfortably.

Dibble was a real experience. I was sixteen years old, star basketball player, baseball pitcher, Future Farmers of America chapter President, had a lovely girlfriend, and I was really "sitting on top of the World". My best friend and I had some great times together, raiding a watermelon field, going to Lindsay and driving up and down Main Street to whistle at girls and exchange talk with the guys and planning stunts to play on others. Also, since Dibble didn't have an organized cemetery crew, the high school boys were often asked to volunteer to dig a grave for a funeral. I did volunteer with two others one day to get out of class. That was the first and last time I dug a grave. We planned two very different tricks, one to get back at one of our class mates who thought he was a super macho man, and one to help a really bashful guy win a girlfriend. I am happy to share these stories with you. The first one I called:

The Phantom of Hanging Tree Creek

Outside of Dibble, on a gravel road there is a small creek with a large oak tree which was used to hang two cattle rustlers in earlier times. According to the indisputable testimony of an outstanding citizen, the ghosts of the two men still haunt the area. This was really good news for the guys who liked to take their girls to the area and "protect" them from the ghosts, while getting a good excuse to hold the girl and do a little romancing. The story is that when the car crosses the bridge and stops, a large white hand will appear on the back window, the car may gently rock a little, and some moans and groans will be heard. The expectation of these events usually resulted in closer snuggling and promises of protection. What fun. I am not convinced that the girls believed the story, but it was a good excuse for both parties. Now the stage is set for my friend and I to have some fun.

I heard macho man bragging about his approaching date with a girl from Lindsay, a nearby town, who had not heard of the hangings and haunting before, so he was going to take her to the hanging tree and make out with her. I told my friend and we began to plan how to make this a memorable event for the guy and gal. We were going to be the ghosts. On the day of macho man's date, we went to the bridge early and pulled his van into the woods where it couldn't be seen and waited for dark. Soon after it was dark, we heard a car approaching and got behind some bushes to hide. It was macho man and his date. Christmas had come early for us because we were really going to enjoy ourselves. We waited for things to progress before we moved. As we sneaked in close to the car, we heard him telling the story of the Hanging Tree and how it was supposed to be haunted there, but if the ghosts did show up, he would protect her. We decided the time had come to start the show. Since my friend's hands were larger than mine, he was going to provide the hand on the back window and I would provide the shaking and moans. He had thought to bring along some flour so that the white hand would stand out better. When the "necking" was going well, the big white hand was placed on the window, and I began to moan and shake the car. At first there was no reaction because the cuddling and kissing were getting hotter. I shook the car harder and moaned louder, and I saw macho man look up and glance in the rearview mirror. He did a double take, gasped, and tried to start his car. Being nervous, he had to try three times before it started. His girl was shaking and making noises, but hadn't screamed. Macho man tried to put the car in gear, but only succeeded in grindings the gears. He tried another gear and when it engaged he took off, spinning his wheels and throwing gravel behind him like a hail storm. He must have been traveling at fifty miles per hour within a quarter of a mile. My friend and I were rolling on the ground, laughing so hard our sides were hurting. When we got ourselves together, we got the van out of the trees and drove into Lindsay to have a hamburger and coke and then back to Dibble. The next day we saw macho man, and asked how his date with the new girlfriend had gone. Did he take her to Hanging Tree Creek? Did they see any ghosts? Did he have a good time? Did he plan to take another girl there? We told him that if he had been really successful that we would try it out with our girls. He never answered a single question. Now what could have caused him to remain silent?

This second prank was not as funny as the other, and when it was over, we felt bad about it. It involved three basketball players, one other boy and our basketball coach. Coach was not a whole lot older than we were, but he should have had more sense. This episode is called:

The Bashful Beau

It seems that in every town, fraternity, group or clique there is at least one person who is extremely shy. One such boy in our senior class was like this. As graduation time was approaching, the bashful beau was concerned that he wouldn't have a date for the Senior party. Not a prom because there were only twelve in our class, four boys and eight girls, and no real facility for a prom anyway. None of the girls in our class were approached by Beau for some reason. We talked with our coach and he said that we could do a prank that might help the guy get the nerve to ask one of the class mates to the party. Well, he was older and, we thought, wiser, so we went along with the plan which involved quite a bit of planning and time. This was the plan. Coach knew of an abandoned house on a country road that still look lived in. He said we were to get the Beau and tell him we knew of a girl who was as bashful as he was, and wanted to meet a boy and that we would drive him to her house and he could talk with her. Meanwhile, Coach would precede us to the house, go inside with his shotgun, and prepare to scare the Beau out of his wits, or give him courage. Beau was really excited because he was looking forward to meeting someone who felt like he did. We told him we would talk with the girl and set up a date for him to meet her. This was on a Thursday and we waited until Friday to tell Beau about the date to be on Saturday night. I imagine Beau was in a pretty agitated state all day Saturday. Finally, when it was dark, about 8:00 p.m., we picked Beau up and drove him to the house. We told him we didn't want to alarm the girl so we stopped about a block from her house and he got out to walk so that she would know he was alone. We began to feel a little remorse at our plan, but not quite enough to abandon it. He walked to the house and knocked on the door. From inside the house cane a loud voice shouting "Who in the hell is here after my daughter"? "She is not going out with no grubby country boy ". The window was opened and a shotgun blast filled the air. Beau was scared and shocked, and took off running as fast as he could. We went after him with the car, but he must have covered a quarter of a mile before we caught him. When we did catch him, we asked what had happened. We said we heard a gun shot, but didn't realize what was happening until we saw him running down the road. He told us the story, and we took him back home. Because of his trust in us, we never told him about the prank and our part in the whole plot. We really felt bad, and this was the only prank that we regretted because it did not turn out funny and we had caused more hurt to Beau. We vowed never to do such a thing again. I would like to blame the coach for leading us into such an outcome, but we were to blame as much as anyone.

Dibble was the last place where I did really physical, hard, farm work, and where I definitely made up my mind that I would not farm for a living. As an example, the Summer following graduation from High School, Eulas and I got a contract to haul a load of hay to the State Mental Hospital at Norman, Oklahoma.

It was Summer, the temperature was about 95 degrees, and we had to stack the hay in Quonset style barns that were about 20 feet tall close to the top, where the temperature was well over 100 degrees. We finished the load, but didn't do any more that day. The hay was Alfalfa, about twice the weight of grass hay. As soon as I graduated (Salutatorian), from high school, I enrolled at Oklahoma University in Pre-Med. I I soon found out that I couldn't afford to go to medical school because I had no scholarships no money, and student loans were not available yet. Also, I made a D in German which was unacceptable. I changed my major to Education, and transferred to Southeastern State College in Durant, where I stayed with my Aunt Ina. This was about the only way I could start College until I could find a job. I finally found a job at the Eat-N-Ease Restaurant, working from 4:00 p.m. until 12:00 midnight on week nights, and until 2:00 a.m. Saturday Night. Despite the hours and the difficulty in finding study time, I managed to pass all my courses. I had moved from my Aunt's home after I found the job, and I stayed at a boarding house where I paid a whole $30.00 a month rent, and got two meals, breakfast and supper, except I didn't always get supper because of having to work. After my brother, Bill got out of the Air Force and started to College at Oklahoma A&M I moved up there to finish school and stayed with him and his wife, Pat. I helped out with housework and also worked two jobs at the College. I worked in the Audio-Visual Center, showing films to different classes as they were scheduled, and cleaning and splicing films that were broken. I also was the Janitor at the Science Building. It only took about three hours in the evening to sweep and empty trash baskets, and dust the classrooms and offices. With this work, and staying with Bill and Pat, and having some help from Mom and Dad in buying groceries, we managed to complete school. I finished in August, 1955, and was hired to teach in Wichita, Kansas to start in September, 1955, so I did not go through the ceremony until May, 1956. Bill actually finished in May, 1956, so we both went through the ceremonies at the same time.

Dad had been hired as Principal of the school in Earlsboro, Oklahoma prior to my move to Stillwater and Oklahoma A&M. The first Summer after they moved to Earlsboro, I took a break from college and spent the summer at home. I got a job working at a fireworks warehouse in Shawnee. I met a girl working there whose home was in Earlsboro. After a few days we began to talk about a big Fourth of July party at her house and began to buy many different kinds of fireworks, like rockets, roman candles, spark spewing fountains, and fire crackers. When the Fourth arrived, we met at her house and set things up for the big show. We were safety conscious, so we set up a metal tub to put the ground fireworks on and had water nearby in case of a grass fire. Friends and family were seated in front of our display so that they could see all the action. We had put our box of fireworks behind the tub, and when it got dark, we started the show. First the sky rockets, then the roman candles, and the fire spewing fountains. The first one we set up was called Mount Vesuvius. It was spectacular, and "oohs and aahs" were heard from the crowd. A sudden gust of wind blew the fountain over, and it spewed is contents into our box of fireworks. Now we really had a grand display. Rockets, chasers, fountains, all were ignited and began to shoot all over the place. People were scattering to avoid being hit by a rocket or a chaser, and the more stationary fireworks were creating a wonderful display of color and noise. It really was great, but was over too quickly. After things settled down a little, we opened the soft drinks and snacks and began to recover from the excitement. No one was hurt, but we did hear a lot of talk about the exciting event and how much fun it was, after the initial shock.

I close this with a tragedy that happened at the warehouse. One of the workers was carrying a box of fireworks on his shoulder and dropped them. They exploded, killing him and destroying the building. The result was devastating. The Company never recovered from the loss.

Chapter Two

Married

Sometimes we think things are "planned" and we have no idea why or how, but the way I met Mary was certainly preordained or we would not have met. Too many things had to come together to be accidental as you will see when I tell you how Mary and I met. During Spring Break from Oklahoma A&M, I went home to my parents in Earlsboro, Oklahoma. I was in my Senior year of College, and was looking forward to some rest and fun. I went downtown and as I was walking along, I saw this girl that was very attractive, and I knew I had to meet her. Since my younger Brother Bob worked in the local grocery store, I figured he would know who she was. He did. He said she was with her friend, Jesse De Lao, who was the daughter of Mrs. Orr who lived in town, and they were visiting her. He said that Jesse had invited him to go with them to Shawnee to go skating. I told Bob to ask if I could go also. Bob was reluctant to ask, so I made him an offer he couldn't refuse, ask, or I would break his arm. Naturally, I won out. He called Jesse and told her his older brother was home from college, and wanted to go with the group to Shawnee. Jesse said sure. I went, and skated with Mary all evening, a good reason to hold her hand and put my arm around her waist. After we left the skating rink, I told Mary about our Church having a picnic at the little lake on Saturday, and asked her to come. She agreed and this was the start of a very long relationship. After we had eaten, I walked her around the lake and kissed her for the first time. Later I took her to Mrs. Orr's house, and asked her to watch the softball game the church was having after church on Sunday. She said she would be there. After the game, we were talking and she said they were leaving the next day to go back to San Antonio, Texas. I promised her I would write, and my letter almost beat her home. I didn't find out until after we were married that I was a goner. She told Jesse on the way home "that is the man I am going to marry". She knew things that were going to happen before they did happen. We wrote letters to each other, and when it came time for the National Guard to go to Fort Hood for training, I was really happy to go. La Vona lived in San Antonio, and would let me stay with them for a few days. Without a car, not much dating to be done, but we managed to spend a lot of time together. Before I had to leave to go back to Stillwater, I gave her my Highschool ring as a promise ring, although I didn't know at the time that was what it was called. Back in Stillwater, I went to Zale's Jewelers and bought a wedding set, on time, since I wasn't rich. We wrote back and forth and finally we had Christmas break. I said hi to Mom and Dad, and took off for San Antonio and Mary. After I got my nerves under control, I asked her formally to marry me, she said yes, and we talked about a date. My semester ended about the middle of May, so we set the date for June 3, 1955. I gave her the engagement ring, sealed with a long kiss. After a couple of days, I had to go back to Stillwater for my final class for my B.S. degree. She and Jesse became very busy planning and sewing and all that makes a wedding happen. Meantime, I had interviewed with the School Superintendent of Wichita, Kansas ISD, and was hired to start in September, 1955.

After this "whirlwind" courtship of one year, actually we saw each other about six weeks total time during this year, we were married in the Foursquare Gospel Church in San Antonio Texas, on June 3, 1955. I was 21 years old and Mary was 20 years old. I think the time was about 7:00 p.m. We had a beautiful wedding. Joe Smith, my Brother-in-law at the time, was best man, and my Dad was witness and Groomsman, and nervous. Mary said her Dad, who gave her away, was also nervous. Maybe they were just excited about getting the two of us out of their hair. Following the wedding, there was the picture taking session while Grace, Mary's sister, and my sister La Vona, and others set up the reception in the church annex. We had the usual ceremonies of throwing the garter and bouquet, cutting the cake, etc., and then we took off. We were going to go to Mary's home and change clothes and then go to the Gunter Hotel for our first night together. There was only one problem. We had forgotten the key to the house, so we pulled the screen off the front window, and Mary crawled through the window, in her wedding dress to open the door. We had to get up early and head for Oklahoma because I still had one course of study in College to finish to get my Degree in Education and qualify for a Kansas Teaching Certificate. We had bought a 1952 Chevrolet 4 door car. It was packed and ready to go. The only thing I will say about our first night, it was wonderful.

We left San Antonio early the next morning and drove to Matoy, Oklahoma, which is not too far from Durant, Oklahoma, and spent the day and night with my Grandmother Tidwell. She was excited to see us and we had a great few hours with her before we left for Stillwater, and Oklahoma A&M College. We had rented an apartment that had been made by converting a garage into a one bedroom, bath, and living, dining, and kitchen area all in one. The address was 517 1/2 Duck Street. Bill, my brother, and Pat, his wife, had "prepared" our first home for us by short-sheeting the bed, and putting a few cracker crumbs in the bed. They had thought we would get in late at night and jump in bed and then become frustrated by the short-sheet, etc. We fooled them, however, by getting in early in the afternoon. We discovered the setup, and fixed them before night came. The next day, I had to report to class, and to my job in the Audio-Visual Center, where I ran projectors for classes who needed movies, and also spliced broken films, cleaned them, etc., which earned me a huge fifty cents an hour. Fortunately, the rent on our apartment was only $30.00 a month. Even this amount caused us to really have to pinch the pennies. Tuna was cheap, as well as pot pies, and we ate a lot of tuna casseroles and pot pies. Mary did her best at making palatable dishes from these sources, and we did survive in good health.

One unforgettable event I have to relate is this. We were discussing what to have for dessert one day, and I suggested a pie. I don't remember what kind of pie, but Mary said that we didn't have a rolling pin to roll out the crust. We discussed it back and forth, and I said, "Why don't you use a vinegar bottle as a rolling pin?" Mary was a little put out with me by that time, and her response: "I'll make the pie if I have to roll out the crust with my head"! The pie was delicious. Most of the days were class, work, and study for me. Our social life consisted of visits to Bill and Pat, movies, and enjoying each other's company.

The months of June and July passed rather quickly, and before we knew it, it was time to leave to Wichita, Kansas where I had a contract to teach school. I had interviewed with a representative of Wichita School District while still in school and was hired to start in September, 1955. We drove to Wichita, Kansas and arrived there pretty early. We got a newspaper and a map of the city, and began to hunt for an apartment that we could afford. We finally found one on North Rutan, a story and half duplex. We moved in rather quickly because we didn't have much to move, just clothing, bed linens, and some kitchen and eating materials. Little did we know what was in store for us.

Neither Mary or I are easily "spooked", and we are not ones to go around talking about ghosts and spirits, but let me tell you before the end of the first week, there was no doubt in our minds that something evil was in the apartment. When you entered the apartment, you came into the living area, passed into the dining area and then the kitchen in the back. The bedroom was up a half flight of stairs, which made it the half story apartment. The first night we went up the stairs and felt something a little strange, but attributed it to being the first night in a strange house. The second night the feeling was a little stronger, and by the third night, wow! As I walked up the stairs, I felt something sort of cool, the third step I felt a definite presence, and by the time I reached the top the hair on the back of my neck was standing straight up or out. Mary and I looked at each other, turned around and went back downstairs and took the cushions off the sofa and slept on the floor of the living room. The next day,

I pulled the mattress from the bed and hauled it down to the living room where we slept for the next twenty-seven days. We had to stay that long because we had already paid the rent, and we couldn't afford to move until I had my first paycheck from the school system. We had no problems with the lower level of the apartment. We could not feel the presence or sense of any evil thing, or any reason to be afraid. When we moved out at the end of the month, the landlady said "I don't know why I can't keep the apartment rented for more than a month". We could have told her, but we didn't because we didn't want to be looked on as weird.

We moved to another apartment on Morris Street, which was closer to the school where I was teaching.

The school was MacArthur Elementary and was close to the Boeing air field where they were working on the development of the JATO, Jet Assisted Take Off, planes. These were propeller driven planes that had some pods that were used to supply jet power to help the bombers take off on shorter runways. The noise was terrible and they were taking off and landing frequently. Mary had gotten a job at Sears, which was about two blocks from our apartment, and with two incomes, we were "better off". Having moved to Wichita in August, we were just a couple of months away from cold weather. We were waiting for the first snow, and the fun that goes with winter. Because of the small apartment, we did not have a washing machine, so our laundry was done in the sink and the clothes were hung on the enclosed porch to dry. Our entertainment consisted of reclining on the couch and listening to the radio. We listened to "Gunsmoke", "Inner Sanctum", "Mr. District Attorney", and others. We also read and went to the movies. Our best remembrances of going to the movies in the winter was coming home, baking a pan of gingerbread, and eating it hot, with lots of butter and coffee. Very tasty.

We parked the car on the side of the apartment close to our bedroom window, and one morning, we woke up and I looked out the window and saw a big mound of snow. During the night it had snowed and about covered the car. This caused us to get up earlier and I had to leave for school earlier than normal because of the traffic conditions. Mary had to walk to Sears to work because she didn't have to be at work as early as I did. I was glad it was not too far from home. I would pick her up at night when she worked late shifts. We had a lot of fun in Wichita, and look back on those times as being the basis for our 61+ years of marriage.

Visiting our parents involved travel. My parents lived in central Oklahoma, which was about 250 miles from Wichita so visiting them didn't require a long drive. Mary's parents lived in San Antonio, and that was about 650 miles away. That required a lot of driving. We would leave Wichita on Friday afternoon after school, and drive until we got to San Antonio, about 16 hours later. We would get into San

Antonio about 2:00 a.m. the following morning. We would not attempt any such trip now.

An amusing incident happened on one of our trips to visit my parents in Lindsay. The Kansas Highway Patrol had set up a driver's license checkpoint. When we stopped, I gave the Patrolman my Oklahoma driver's license. He asked where we lived and I told him in Wichita, Kansas where I was a school teacher. He checked the license plates and saw they were from Texas. He looked rather puzzled, so I explained that I had grown up in Oklahoma, had married in San Antonio, Texas, and had been hired to teach school in Wichita. He kind of shook his head and mumbled to himself, Oklahoma driver's license, Texas License plates, and lives in Kansas. He looked at us, smiled, and said drive carefully.

April, 1956, at the age of 22 years, I received a letter from the U.S. Government which started out: Greetings, you are ordered to report to Kansas City, Missouri, for a physical examination prior to induction into the United States Army. I went, I passed, and then I called the Draft Board to see if I could enter the Army from San Antonio as Mary would stay there while I was in the service of our Country. They said I could, so in May, after school was out, we packed up and moved to San Antonio. We were talking about how we accumulate things and as an example; when we left San Antonio for Stillwater, we packed everything in the trunk of the car. When we left Stillwater, we had stuff in the trunk, and also in the back seat of the car. When we moved from Wichita, Kansas to San Antonio, Texas, we had the trunk of the car full, the back seat full and level with the top of the front seats, and we had shipped several boxes ahead. We arrived in San Antonio and moved in with Mary's parents. I got a temporary job for the summer and Mary went to work for Frost National Bank. My temporary job was arranged by my sister, Mary Lou, at Russ and Company, an investment firm. I had the pleasure of being the "gofer", and Address-o-graph machine operator for the couple of months before entering the Army. About July, Mary discovered she was pregnant which was great news, but I was going to be in the Army during her pregnancy and child birth.

Married With Children

I did not mention the children in the first part of "Married" as I wanted to tell more of the childhood of Alan and Mark. They were ten years apart in age, so, essentially, we raised two "only child" children. For us, it was better because the expenses of raising them was spread out and our finances were not unduly hit, but for them, it was not possible fore them to develop the close relationship that I had with my siblings in their younger years.

Alan was a year old when I came home from Germany, and it took him a bit of time to get close to me as his father. The man in his life was Morris, Mary's brother, who helped out with caring for him. Mary's, other brother, Merle, was in college at the University of California, Los Angeles, completing his B.S. degree in Electrical Engineering, and her sister, Grace was in the Four Square Bible College, earning her degree in Theology, also in Los Angeles, California. When Merle finished, he was employed by General Electric to work on Radar equipment that was "strung" along the coast of Florida, the Bahamas, then into Europe, in several Countries, including Spain, Germany, France and some smaller Countries. He was there about the time of my last year in Germany. He became sick with some problem and was sent to the U.S. Military Hospital in Frankfurt, Germany. He recovered and then was sent back to the U.S.

Back to my Boys. Alan was still wearing diapers when I got home and we took the 2 weeks to travel and enjoy our vacation time. This was before dependable paper diapers, so we used cloth diapers, which had to be washed and dried. Lightly soiled diapers were washed at a service station and then hung out of the car window to dry as we drove to our next destination. I have no idea what people thought as we drove merrily on our way.

On his second birthday, we bought him a cowboy hat, boots, toy pistol, and a metal rocking horse. He really enjoyed the outfit. (I still have his horse in the attic). Alan was always "head strong" and demanding as this next story will show. We had Morris, Grace and Mary's mother with us in the car, driving to Medina Lake for the afternoon. Alan wanted some chewing gum, which we did not have, and he started to fuss and carry on. We tried to tell him there was no place to stop and buy gum. He kept fussing about it until we reached the lake and then he finally became interested in the rocks and rock casts of the large clams that live in the lake and things became a lot better.

When he was five years old, I began to teach him firearm safety. We had some rifles at home and we did not want him to "play" with them, so I took him to the ranch and began to teach him how to handle a rifle. First I bought him a BB gun and showed him how to cock it, aim at a target, and shoot it. He was a quick learner and did not mishandle the gun. After some time, over the next few weeks of shooting at large targets, I hung some wooden clothes pins of the line and had him shoot at them. H quickly learned how to hit them, and didn't miss the pins very often. When I felt he was ready, and observing how he handled the BB gun, I took the single shot .22 cal. Rifle to the ranch and began to show him how to use it properly, stressing how much more dangerous it was. By showing him how the .22 bullet could damage tin cans, boards, and other objects, he grasped that it was not to be shot carelessly, and certainly not to point it at people or things he did not, or should not, shoot. He became a good shot with it, and this knowledge helped him earn a Merit Badge in the Boy Scouts years later. Alan finished high school. Went to San Antonio College and received a degree in construction. He started working for Ray Ellison, home builder/developer, and really learned great additional ways to do wood work, carpeting, home plumbing, etc.

He met a young lady by the name of Carrie Williams, and they married June 20, 1982. In !984, Jessica Rene was born in San Antonio. Shortly after that, Alan went in to the Army. He was sent to Electronics school to learn how to install and operate radar tracking dishes, for the satellite program being developed for the military and space programs. While stationed in Georgia, Anthony Brian was born on March 11, 1987. Alan was then assigned to the Satellite Tracking operation in Washington D.C. When he was to be discharged, he was contacted and hired by the USAA Insurance Company created for military members, both active duty and retired/separated veterans of the Armed Forces. USAA was informed by Alan's Father-in--law, James Williams who was employed with USAA, of Alan's training and work. USAA was preparing to use satellite tracking for their insurance program as they are World Wide. Alan was sent a plane ticked and given an interview date. He was hired and the family was moved to San Antonio. He has been with USAA for 25 years, and plans to retire in October,

2020. Jessica married Matthew Thibodeaux on 1-29-08. They had one child, Alexis Violet born 4-15-2009, the only Great Grand Child at this time. Tony has not yet found the girl he wants to marry.

Mark Timothy, born May 8, 1967, graduated from high school, went to St. Philips College in the Vocational Nursing Program, graduated and was hired by the Baptist Hospital System as a Nurse. He wants to complete the Nurse Practitioner degree also. Mark also received training in using firearms, as did Alan, and also earned a Merit Badge in Boy Scouts, where he earned the rank of Eagle Scout, the first one in the family. Alan achieved the rank of Life Scout, but went into the Explorer program and did not try for Eagle Scout.

Mark met his future wife, Vivian Mohn, while in college and they married 8-15-1992. Mark enrolled in Bible College and earned a degree in Theology. He and Vivian started off in rather dire circumstances. Mark was still in school, as was Vivian, and they lived in a trailer house. Both sets of parents helped them out until they began to have an income. Jan. 30, 1998, Vivian gave birth to Esther Mary, and with her degree in Education, began teaching school. Good for Mary and I as we got to baby sit Esther. Mark had changed to Nursing instead of Theology, and began working at the South East Baptist Hospital as a Nurse and was also an Emergency Med. Tech, and flew on the helicopters as the flight nurse after completing his LVN nursing courses. He has completed the requirements for a B.S. Degree for R.N. in Nursing, and is going to get a Nurse Practitioner degree. On 9-9-2000, Vivian gave birth to Mark Timothy II. They didn't want a Junior. On October 24, 2003, Vivian gave birth to Ezekiel Caleb. I have really enjoyed all the 5 Grand Children. Mark has worked all his years of Nursing, in the E.R., and as an EMT flight Nurse. He has worked in both the Pediatric ER and the Adult ER. He sometimes fills in for the Pastor at Church when the Pastor is absent. Following the death of Mary, Mark inherited the 80 acres and mixes a bit of ranching in his activities. Actually, it is 78.79 acres of land. A couple of years ago, he and his friends talked about building a shooting range. One of the men bought a large metal shipping container and had it moved to the ranch. The men then bought building material and built an upper and lower deck, complete with shooting benches, over the container, and built dirt berms for 300 yards and 100 yards range, and a pistol range of 25 and 50 feet.

Ester is currently working at Chick-Filet as a shift leader. She has been working there for several years. Ester has not met the man she would marry, but I feel she will one of these days. She and Mark T. have started going to another church where most of their friends are going which leaves Ezekiel and Mark as the music providers at Red Bird Church the first two Sundays of each month. Ezekiel does work for the

Pastor on the grounds of the Church to earn some money. At this time, Mark T. is between jobs. Maybe, before I finish this book, I will be able to tell about his new work.

Update To Married

In 2006, we went a little wild in spending. We bought a new Silverado pickup since the old Ford had almost 500k miles, and needed constant service and small repairs. Later, we bought a 2006 Chevy Tahoe. Altogether, we spent about $45,000 on both vehicles. Sadly, in 20012, an idiot driver rear ended us in the Silverado, and the insurance company totaled it. However, we bought a 2012 Silverado, and enjoyed the benefits of better transportation and comfort.

Grace, Mary's sister, developed cancer on her pancreas in late 2012, and after several months of treatment and hospice care, she passed away in March, 2013.

September, 2013 brought terrible news for us. Mary had been having quite a bit of pain and problems with her Urinary system, so She went to Dr. Joan Meany, Urologist, and through the use of the cystoscope, she found that Mary had a rather large tumor in her bladder. The tumor was growing across the ureter on her Right kidney. Blocking the flow of urine/waste products from the kidney. Mary was admitted to the Methodist hospital for surgery using the cystoscope as the access to the tumor. Dr. Meany was able to re-sect most of the tumor, but some of it was embedded into the wall of the bladder, and could not be removed without removing the bladder, which Mary refused to have happen. Dr. Meaney recommended Chemotherapy and referred Mary to Oncology Group of San Antonio. Dr. Jaffar referred her to Dr. Robinson for the installation of a port, so that chemo could be done without accessing a vein each time. Mary endured chemo once a week from 2013 to late 2015, when Dr. Jaffar took her off chemo because she could not tolerate the stress of chemo any longer. During the course of chemo, Mary had to have numerous blood transfusions, which were an ordeal in themselves. Mary became weaker, and had more difficulty in walking, finally, we obtained a wheel chair from Mark, our son, so that Mary could get out more and be more mobile. In late January, Mary became weaker, and in more pain, more difficulty in breathing, etc., so our Family Dr., Brian Senger referred her to Vitas Hospice. Mary insisted on in-home hospice services, which started the first part of February. She was provided a hospital bed, oxygen, bed pads, etc., and daily visits from the Nurse and nurse aide. I continued to prepare her meals, change her bed linen, bathe her, etc. During the last week of her life, although we didn't know it was her last week, I slept in her room on a roll-away bed so that I could be near her. On February 10, 2016, I prepared Mary for bed, fixed her bed and pads, fixed the nebulizer to help her breathe a little better, and finally kissed her and turned off the light.

She was having some breathing difficulty, but drifted off to sleep. This was about 10:00 p.m. I lay down on the roll-away, and dozed off. About 1:00a.m., I woke up to check on her and I did not hear her breathing. I knew then that she had passed away, so I got up, checked on her and she was cold to the touch, and was not breathing. Sometime between 10:00p.m. And 1:00 a.m., she had silently passed away. I called the Hospice nurse and she came as quickly as possible. She pronounced her death as 3:08 a.m., February 11, 2016. She called Simplicity Funeral Home, and they picked up her body about 1 hour later. Alan went with me to the funeral home to drop off her burial clothes and then to San Jose Burial Park to arrange for opening the grave and arranging graveside service chairs and canopy. Mary had arranged for the songs and with Mark to lead the service, she was interred on February 18, 2016. God, how I miss her.

Since Mary has passed away, I have been spending more time with Mark and family and Alan and Family. They are helping me to keep my resolve to keep active and involved. I have started going to Red Bird Ranch Church with Mark. I have really enjoyed the fellowship and teaching of the Pastor, and just being involved in something else meaningful to my life. I have also connected with my sisters on a more frequent level through the use of my new Computer and Facebook. I still go to the ranch to check on the cattle and I enjoy having something to do.

Chapter Three

Army Service

Now begins my military experience, which took place when I was 23-25 years old. This period of time was 1956 -1958. In September, I was finally called to report to the induction center for the Army and was sent to Fort Bliss in El Paso, Texas. There I was shorn of my hair, given my uniforms, which didn't fit, and several days of testing. If ever a name was misleading, it was Ft. Bliss. Nothing blissful about it, hot, dry, sandy and a long way from home. After about two weeks, we were sent to Fort Hood, Texas, for our basic training. We were part of an experiment by the Army, wherein we received accelerated training and in six months we would be ready to be moved to Germany to replace the 2nd Armored Division. I was assigned to the 279th Battalion, Company A, of the 3rd Armored Division. Having had almost six years of training in the National Guard of Oklahoma, and having reached the rank of Sargent First Class, I was made Acting Platoon Sergeant when I reached

Fort Hood, and this got me out of K.P. duty and a lot of other menial chores. I was also given the dubious honor of having two tanks assigned to me, and I was the Tank Commander. We enjoyed sitting on top of the tanks as we traveled to and from the training area, waving to the Infantry who were hiking along. It was at Fort Hood that I learned the value of two "female" items, Kotex and Jergens Lotion. During the winter, the weather was really rough on the hands. The cold and dry winds, water, and elements would chap the skin, to the point of cracking and bleeding. Mary saw my hands on one of my weekend passes home, and got me a bottle of Jergens hand lotion. I took it back to Fort Hood, and received quite a bit of ribbing about using hand lotion for women. In a couple of days, my hands had healed and were protected from further chapping. Needless to say, a lot of Jergens was bought from the PX by the rest of the Platoon. As part of the training, we had to crawl on our hands and knees under barbed wire, in ditches, and over little hills while machine guns were firing overhead and small charges of dynamite were set off to simulate artillery fire, called "the confidence course". In order to protect my knees and elbows, I bought a box of Kotex and tied them around my elbows and knees. They served two purposes, protected my uniform and padded my knees and elbows so that I could get through the course faster. A lot of Kotex was bought in the PX by others so that they could also enjoy the protection and padding.

Training was accelerated. I was made Tank Commander, which meant that I was in charge of the tank and crew. Within the first three weeks, we had fired every weapon in the tank company, pistols, rifles, carbines, .45 cal. "grease gun", an automatic weapon, the .30 cal. machine gun, and the .50 cal. machine gun. The fun came in firing the .90mm tank gun. It was a real blast, literally. We learned to drive the tanks, and operate the guns and equipment associated with the tanks. Within 6 weeks, we were on maneuvers practicing tank warfare tactics. Believe me, the training was so intense that we would collapse at night, and sleep through anything. I slept on rocks and never felt them. I slept through a repair on a tank that was rolling back and forth about 3 feet from my feet, and never heard a thing. The first thing we were told about tanks was how safe they were, thick steel and other safety features. The next day, we were told of the many ways a tank could be stopped, disabled, and the danger of armor piercing bullets.

I was fortunate while at Fort Hood to be given weekend passes home. Mary was pregnant with Alan and it was great to be with her at least on weekends. She was still working at Frost Bank.

In March 1957, Mary went to the hospital with labor pains. Our good friend, Jessie De Lao, took her to the hospital and had the Red Cross call my Unit to request a deferment from shipping out to Germany until after the birth of the baby, and request that I be given leave to be with Mary. She had a rare blood type, RHB Negative. This could cause complications with the birth of the baby, so I was given leave time to come home. In addition, the Division had been given orders to depart the first week of April, 1957, to Friedberg, Germany, to complete the rotation of entire Divisions. Because of the recent birth of Alan, I was given 30 days deferment to stay in Fort Hood, so I didn't go to Germany until May, 1957

I left Fort Hood, by train, to travel to Brooklyn Army Terminal in Brooklyn, New York. We took the scenic route, through Louisiana, Mississippi, Alabama, Georgia, South Carolina, North Carolina, Virginia,

Pennsylvania and into New York. There we were loaded onto the ship and assigned living quarters. Traveling apart from my Division, I was assigned to Special Duty. I was part of a group of people who performed various duties on the ship to make the travel more pleasant. I was the Ship's "D.J." I got to sit in a studio and play music all day, piped throughout the ship. The only incident which caused me any problem was the first morning out I decided to wake everyone with Chuck Berry's song which started "Up in the Morning, and off to School". A rather loud and jazzy song which tended to jangle the nerves. A message was passed along to the DJ room that we WOULD NOT play such music so early to wake up the passengers, particularly the officers and their families. In between records, we would play poker. I was able to win enough money to keep me going in Germany until I received my first pay check. I had left all the money I had, except for about $10.00 with Mary.

The trip across was pretty bumpy. The ship did a lot of up and down motion, and some side to side rolls. I was fortunate not to get sea sick, but I did come close one time. We ate standing up in the mess hall of the ship. Chairs would have to have been bolted down and that would have caused maintenance problems. If the seas were a little high, the trays of food would slide back and forth if you didn't hold on to the tray. One morning, it was particularly rough, and the ship was rolling from side to side more than usual. One of the men was sort of queasy to begin with, and looking at the mess of scrambled eggs and stuff, he couldn't take it anymore, and threw up in his tray. He let go of the tray and it slid down the table while the rest of us lifted our trays out of the way. The sight of the tray with a mixture of food and vomit was too much for most of the guys, and almost too much for me. I did not finish breakfast however. We landed in Bremerhaven, Germany, 16 days after leaving New York. I joined my Division in Friedberg, Germany and was promptly assigned to Battalion Headquarters. Never mind the expensive training I had had in tanks. Because I could type, and had the B.S. Degree, they thought I would be more valuable in Battalion Headquarters. I never saw the inside of a tank again.

My duties consisted of typing letters, orders, transcripts of Article 15 violations (Company Punishment), without any prison time. I also wrote letters or Memoranda of Commendation. These were the flowery communication that bragged on the soldier, and looked good in the records. I became a master of flowery phrases and general B.S., and developed a fairly imaginative vocabulary which helped me out in civilian life.

We had monthly "alert" drills. During the night, sirens would sound, we would all get dressed and head for our duty stations. Since I worked in Battalion Headquarters, we would load all the files, records, and field office equipment in the back of a truck, and then follow the Colonel wherever the practice said to go. We saw quite a lot of Germany this way. We learned after the first drill to stop at the mess hall and grab some coffee before leaving. We also obtained a small burner which used Sterno, to make our own coffee. We would be out all day, driving around and killing time. Back at Headquarters, we unloaded the stuff, and then went to the Enlisted Men's Club, to unwind after such a strenuous work day. All in all, the duty was very good, no stress, except being away from home.

Now for the off-duty time. Fred, Walt, Tom, and I all worked in Headquarters. I was the S-1 Clerk, Tom was S-2 clerk, Fred was S-3 clerk, and Walt handled the Motor pool paper work. S-1 was the Commanding Officer, S-2 was Communications, S-3 was Intelligence. We developed a pretty close friendship, and when possible, we planned leave time together. We worked it out with Headquarters for all four of us to take leave at the same time. Walt had bought a used Opel car, and we chipped in to buy gasoline vouchers to use "on the economy", which meant off base. We had two weeks so we planned a tour of Europe, most of it any way. We left our base and drove to Munich first, where we stopped at the biggest Bier Garten, had a few cold ones, the drove around the City looking at the attractions. From there we went to Austria, looking for the Sound of Music locale, but didn't find it. Next was Switzerland, then across the Alps into Italy. The first night in Italy was spent in a small Bed and Breakfast house in Verona, Italy. We went to Venice next, took the Gondola rides, walked along the canals, enjoyed the atmosphere and the people. The next was Rome.

We stopped on top of one of the Seven Hills and took pictures of Rome, old and new. Next, we went to the Vatican, visited the museum and Art gallery, then stood in St. Peter's Square, which is really round. There we met a young man with a Cadillac Convertible, who offered us a tour of the

City for $5.00. We visited the Coliseum, the Catacombs, some old temples and ruins, and the Trevi Fountain. If you throw a coin in the fountain, you are supposed to return to Rome. Didn't work for me. From Rome we went to Naples and then around to Sorrento, also on the Bay of Naples. We were doing our traveling in November, off tourist season, so we spent the night in a luxury hotel for only $5.00 each. We were the only guests. We sat on the veranda and watched the lights of ships and the city of Naples, sipping our cold wine. The next morning, we caught the ferry to the Isle of Capri. We visited the Blue Grotto by boat, then did the tourist thing. I bought Mary a pearl ring from there. The next day we drove up the West coast of Italy to Florence where we saw some of the statues by Da Vinci, then to the Flea Market by the Arno River where I bought a sweater because as we went up the coast it got a little cooler. Florence to Genoa, home of Christopher Columbus. Next stop was in Monte Carlo, Monaco, where we gambled in the big casino. After leaving Monaco, Fred became quite ill and we began looking for a doctor. We finally found one in a small town as we traveled up the Lyon River valley toward Paris. The doctor treated Fred for food poisoning, and by the time we reached Paris, Fred was feeling much better. Paris lived up to its billing. We checked into a hotel close to the Eiffel Tower, and was told that we could join the Night Club Tour. We did, and went to 4 clubs had a complimentary drink and saw the floor show in each club. The main one was the Moulin Rouge with a fantastic show. Next day we went to the Eiffel Tower, rode up to the third stage, and really saw Paris. A great view. Unfortunately, as we descended to the ground level, we saw a crowd of people and police all looking up into the girders. We looked, and saw the body of a man that had jumped from the tower, but the wind had blown him into the girders of one of the legs. Paris is where I saw my very first "bidet". What is a bidet? A fixture much like a commode, but shot a stream of water to wash the backside. Finally, our leave time was about over, so we cut across France into Germany and worked our way back to Freidburg, our base. Fourteen days, many miles, lots of history, art, and culture, and the whole trip, about $100.00 each. Never to be repeated at this price again.

The next memorable trip was by Fred and I. Since I was the Battalion clerk, I would type up orders to go to many different places, and we would go to the Rhine Main Airforce Base, ask where they may have a "hop" going, and we would produce the orders, and away we would go. Fred and I got a hop to Birmingham, England and caught a train to London. London is a big town, and lots to see. Buckingham Palace and changing of the Guards, the Tower of London, London Bridge, Piccadilly Circus, the Mounted Guards, shops and pubs. We went to a stage play, "The Bells are Ringing", with Judy Holiday, my first and last live stage show. We left London, went through the Chunnel(a combination of tunnel and English channel), to Belgium and the World Fair. Quite an event, all the exhibits and rides, and masses of people. We saw our first color T.V. there. Back to Freidburg and work. It was getting closer to the end of our tour of duty, and we were excited about getting back home. We got the news that Elvis Presley was going to be one of the replacements. Poor guy, he lived off base, was the Colonel's driver, and really had a tough tour of duty. All of my time in Europe was fascinating. I was able to see so many things I had only read about. To actually stand in the old Roman Forum, visit the Vatican, see the catacombs, the Coliseum where gladiators fought, see the statues and art work of Da Vinci, the glamor and sights of Paris and all the other wonderful sights was quite a wonder for this Oklahoma boy. London and Belgium, and all of Germany were experiences that have never been forgotten. I have been asked if I felt any regrets in taking time and the money to take those trips, but I do not. I knew that I probably would never go back to Europe and I wanted to see what I could while Uncle Sam paid the fare to travel there and back. I do regret that Mary couldn't have been there to enjoy it with me.

Meanwhile back at home, Mary was raising Alan. She would send me pictures of Alan with her letters, and tell about him, so I could see how he was growing. He was about 3 weeks old when I left, and 18 months old when I got back. Mary taught herself to drive because she didn't want to rely on someone else.

I know she had a pretty rough time, trying to take care of Alan by herself, and managing her affairs. She always sounded pretty upbeat in her letters to me, and was looking into the future after I finished my tour in the Army. She saved most of the allotment sent her by the government, and what I could send home so that by the time I got out of the Army, we were able to make the down payment on a house, and furnish it with the furniture without having to use credit. I know of no one better at saving money, or shopping for bargains. She was the best financial manager ever.

In September, 1958, we left Germany and arrived back at the Brooklyn Army Terminal 16 days later. The trip back was a lot worse because I didn't get special duty like before. I had to sleep in stacked bunks, so close together that if you needed to get out of the bunk, the people above had to get out so the bunk could be lifted up. If you were skinny, you didn't have that inconvenience. At last the sixteen day trip back was over. We disembarked at Brooklyn Army Terminal, were taken by bus to New Jersey where we were put on a plane to Fort Chaffee, Arkansas, where I was processed out of the Army and then caught a plane to San Antonio, Mary, Alan, and home, at last.

After I got home, we took a two week vacation to get to know each other again, and traveled into Arkansas and Missouri, and then back home. I applied for teaching jobs at several of the local school districts, and finally I was hired by Harlandale, ISD, to start in October, 1958, teaching the special needs class at the Harlandale Jr. High school. We bought our first house at 302 Adelphia and settled in. I taught in the Harlandale Junior High School for two years and then transferred to Carol Bell Elementary as a 6th grade teacher.

Mary started working at Sears in the Customer Service Department and I started working part time in the sporting goods department. We rocked along until 1964, me teaching and her at Sears, and then she went to work with Dr. Schwarting as an Ophthalmological Assistant. After teaching for 6 years, Mary finally encouraged me to get my Master's Degree and I enrolled in Our Lady of the Lake University. I finished the Master's Degree in 1966, actually two degrees, one in Counseling and one in School Administration and was certified in both fields. The way I worked it was by using Counseling courses as electives for the School Administrator degree and the Administrator courses as electives for the Counseling degree. With my Master's in School Administration, I was given the position of Vice Principal and teacher at Kingsborough Elementary School. After two years at Kingsborough, I was told that job opportunities were available for counselors in the Texas Commission for the Blind, and possibly with the Social Security Disability Determination Division. I also learned that the Vocational Rehabilitation Department of the Texas Education Agency was hiring counselors. In that I was already working with the Texas Education Agency as a teacher, I thought I would have a better chance of working in the Vocational Rehabilitation Division. The reason for changing careers was based on salary. The Principal at Kingsborough was only being paid $8,800.00 per year after 30 years of experience, while the Counseling position at Vocational Rehabilitation started at $9,200.00 per year. I was hired for the Vocational Rehabilitation counseling job, starting September, 1967. The following pages are my recollections of my Rehabilitation career.

Chapter Four

My Years as an Educator

When I received my B.S. In Education in 1955, I was interviewed for a teaching position in Wichita, Kansas. I touched on my first year of teaching in telling about Mary and I in Wichita. I was drafted into the Army and after my discharge, I resumed my teaching career in the Harlandale ISD in San Antonio, Texas, where we lived after my discharge from the Army. It was quite a change from the military to teaching, but I was fortunate to get a position starting in October, 1958 after my discharge from the Army, in September 1958. It was terrific that I was able to obtain a teaching position so quickly. It did allow time for Mary, Alan and I to take two weeks of vacation to get reacquainted after two years of separation.

My first position was teaching the special needs class at the Harlandale Junior High, now called Middle School. After two years in this position, I was transferred to Carroll

Bell Elementary as a 6th grade teacher. Those years were really great. The staff was great and teaching was really fun. Each elementary school had different classes for the gifted, normal, and special needs

Children, and each year the teachers were rotated so that we experienced teaching in all levels. All three groups were challenging because of the different levels of learning. In the gifted class I taught, I had the pleasure of teaching a gifted artist, Gilbert Duran. Gilbert was selected to do the different themed holidays on our room sized bulletin board, which were great. Little did I know then that Gilbert was to become a very noted artist in San Antonio. He had several showings, and his paintings are found in many places in the City. I was given a huge aquarium for the class room which was used for various purposes such as a "soothing" influence, a learning device on reproduction, caring for fish and aquaria, responsibility, since different groups were assigned to care for the fish, feeding them, watching the water level, maintaining the oxygen pump, and removing any debris which might have fallen into the tank. Christmas, and end of the school year was the time when the children were given most of the fish to take home since no one would be available to care for them and feed them. The end of the school year was the opportunity to empty the tank, clean it, and get ready for the next class. We had guppies, neons, tiger barbs, among others, which were prolific breeders so there were plenty of fish to take home. Teaching had a lot of high and not so high moments. Fortunately, none were particularly notably extreme enough to remember clearly.

During this time I was really busy. To supplement my salary, which was pretty low, I worked part time at Sears in the sporting goods department. There was one incident that was a learning experience for the salespeople in the sporting goods department. One customer who came into the department was rather shabbily dressed, had a beard, and looked as if he didn't have a dime in his pockets. Since the regular or fulltime employees were also on commission, they didn't want to wait on the customer because they might miss a big sale and lose the commission. I greeted the customer and told him I would wait on him after I finished completing the sale of my present customer. When I finished, I walked over to him and asked how I could help him. He said he was interested in buying a motor boat. I asked what size, and he wanted the 14' boat with motor and trailer. I showed him our floor model and explained the difference in motors. And asked if he intended to use it for water skiing also, he would need a larger motor. He thought he should have a 75hp motor, but I told him 50hp would be better for this boat,

One of the full-time salesmen wanted me to give him the sale since he was on commission. I said no, you saw him, you ignored him because you didn't want to waste your time on someone who, you thought, wouldn't buy much, if anything, and maybe miss a good sale. When I finished writing up the papers, giving him a title to the trailer, and arranged for him to pick up the outfit, he pulled out a big wad of cash and paid the total bill. As I said, this was a learning experience for all the sales staff. Don't base a decision solely on appearance.

I became a little "political" by being involved with the local chapter of the Texas State Teachers Association and being elected as President of the local Chapter. It was through the efforts of the local chapter, along with other chapters. that caused the School Districts to implement the Social Security program Statewide, since the Districts were not required to withhold Social Security deductions. This was in addition to withholding Teacher Retirement fund deductions.

After teaching and working at Sears, Mary pushed me to obtain my Master's Degree so I could have better opportunities to move up in my career. I enrolled in Our Lady of the Lake University in 1964 in the School administration graduate program. While taking the required courses, I took the courses needed for a Master's degree in Counseling and Guidance as electives, and the education courses as electives for the Counseling Degree. I was able to be Certified in school administration and in Counseling, essentially it was two Masters Degrees at one time. Following my graduation, I was promoted to Vice

Principal at Kingsborough Elementary School in 1966. I was not too happy about the salary, and I didn't see much hope for making much more as the Principal, after nearly 30 years of experience was earning only $8,800.00 a year. At that time, Vocational Rehabilitation was under the State Teachers Association and I heard that they were hiring Counselors for the Rehabilitation program. In that I was certified in Counseling, I applied for a position and was hired. My salary as a Counselor increased to $9,200.00 per year, a significant increase in my income. After 10 years of teaching and being a Vice Principal in the Harlandale District, I started as a Counselor for Vocational Rehabilitation. This didn't exactly end my teaching career. Working in the Hospitals and with the medical community, I was hired to teach Anatomy and Physiology in the Medical Assisting department of the San Antonio College, which lasted several years, and supplemented my salary. I was finally qualified to be called Professor. With the Vocational rehabilitation program being under the Teacher Retirement System, all my teaching experience was added to the V.R. experience, which also gave credit for military service, and additional credit for unused vacation and sick leave hours, allowed me to retire with 45 years of creditable service, a good increase in my retirement annuity.

Chapter Five

Texas Rehabilitation Commission Highlights

My job title was Vocational Rehabilitation Counselor. My salary was $9,200.00 per year, an immediate raise of $400.00 I would work with people who were mentally or physically handicapped, provide job training, if needed, job placement, counseling, and medical services when necessary to assist the person to be able to work in a job compatible with their handicap.

When I reported for work, the Offices were on the 27th floor of the Tower Life Building, also known as the Transit Tower, in San Antonio. Mr. E.H. Stendebach was the Regional Director and was greatly expanding the Vocational Rehabilitation program. Several Counselors and staff were being hired, and the office space in the Tower was not sufficient to house all the new employees. A search was made for new office space, and the Regional Director leased sufficient space at 212B Stumberg street. We moved the offices on October 1, 1967. We had two supervisory units in the office, with a third office housed in the State Mental Hospital, and a fourth group housed in the Victoria Courts, a joint office of the Vocational Rehabilitation program and the Department of Public Welfare, called the Project Office. The Stumberg office was great. I had my own office and a secretary who was shared with another counselor, R.W. (only initials used to protect the identity of the staff). The counselors being hired during this time were of three main groups, school teachers, preachers/ministers, and retired military. (Degrees in Vocational Rehabilitation were not introduced in Texas, at this time). Since the program started under the Texas Education Association, teachers were a primary source of employees for vocational rehabilitation positions. R.W. and I shared a secretary, S.J. S. didn't like R.W. too well, so she tended to do more of my work than his. He finally got a typewriter and did a lot of his own typing. R. was a minister, and tended to be a little head strong, and at times, made rash decisions, which landed him in hot water with his wife. A supervisory position became vacant and R. applied for the position, but was not hired. This upset R. and when a counselor position opened in Kerrville, he asked to be transferred to Kerrville. The Regional Director approved the transfer request and R. went home and told his wife to start packing things so they could move to Kerrville.

Poor R., his wife politely told him that he could move to Kerrville, but she and their daughter were staying in San Antonio. For two years, R. commuted to Kerrville each day until he could get a counselor position back in San Antonio.

November 1967, J.C. came to me as asked if I would be interested in starting a vocational/medical rehabilitation program with the new University of Texas Health Science Center. My interest in medical practices led me to answer "heck yes". As part of establishing the Health Science Center, the Bexar County Commissioners had voted to build a new County hospital in the Medical Center. So, temporarily, S.J. and I had established offices at the old Robert B. Green Hospital down town. We started accepting referrals from the doctors and hospital staff. In addition, I was a "courtesy" Counselor for other counselors in the San Antonio area. This meant that while in the hospital or clinics, I was the counselor in charge of their case. I would make rounds with the Resident Doctors in the Orthopedic department and look mostly at patients who were waiting for an amputation of a leg, or who had been paralyzed from accidents, gunshot wounds, or had been paralyzed as a result of a stroke or head injury. . The Chief Resident was Dr. Robert Bilderback, and the Chief of the Orthopedic Surgery Department was Dr. Charles Rockwood. The Medical School Staff worked closely with doctors in private practice who would visit the hospitals and teach the students, Interns and Residents in

Clinics or classes. This was called the Town and Gown agreement.

Finally, the new hospital opened and S.J. and I moved into the new space. Actually we were in examination rooms. The Orthopedic department added a second doctor, David Green, who specialized in treatment and conditions of the Hand and upper extremities. Just prior to Dr. Green joining the staff, Mary was hired as Secretary in the Orthopedic Department. She was a great asset to them, and really worked hard, scheduling meetings, rotation of Interns and Residents into and out of the Department, communication with other departments, etc. Dr. Rockwood was the Physician in Charge of developing the EMT (Emergency Medical Technician) program in San Antonio. Mary transcribed the Manual to be used in training the EMTs.

Other departments and doctors learned of the value of Vocational Rehabilitation, and I was getting referrals from the Neurology Department, The Urology Department and the Cardiology Department. My caseload of clients was soon numbering over 150 cases. I expanded my office and added another counselor, Secretary, and Administrative Technician. I was able to concentrate just on the clients in the Bexar County Hospital, while P. D. was the Counselor at the Robert B. Green Hospital. We were very successful in getting clients to work following medical treatment.

In 1971, the Regional Director of TRC, decided that the patients/clients could be handled by a counselor from one of the district offices. We closed the hospital offices and I was transferred to the East Field Office, located on New Braunfels Ave., a long way from home, and I was assigned to work the Social Security Caseload. This was a caseload devoted to serving only those persons who were receiving Medicare/Medicaid, and were really severely involved in their physical and/or mental conditions. This was also a great learning opportunity for me, as I became very familiar with Nursing Homes and how they operated. I also became very knowledgeable about the rules and regulations of Social Security. I had a very successful year, and my ability to adjust and carry on resulted in a great surprise for me.

In February, 1972, J.C., Assistant Regional Director, came to me and asked if I would like to be a Supervisor. H. Mc., was going to Austin as a Program Specialist and I took his position as Supervisor of the Welfare Project. I assumed the position on March 1, 1972. My experience in the Medical School, and with the Social Security case load was very helpful since many of the clients were on Medicaid. The project was a joint operation between the Vocational Rehabilitation Division and the Department of Public Welfare, and was located in the Victoria Courts, low rent housing for San Antonio. The offices were actually apartments in the buildings that still had bath tubs in the rest rooms. Our function was to work with the clients to get as many as possible off the Welfare rolls and into employment. The office was pretty dingy and we were crowded, but we managed to work very well. Finally, in 1975 we were able to move our project to 120 N. Mesquite, a new, and much nicer, building. After about 2 years, it was decided that we were doing such a good job that we opened another office of the project on Pleasanton Road. In 1980, the VR/DPW Project was closed due to funding problems, and I moved all my counseling and support staff to the office on Mesquite street. We worked hard, provided lots of services, and rehabilitated a lot of clients. In 1982, for reasons unknown, all the Area Managers, our new title, were called to the Regional Office and told that we were involved in a "fruit basket" turnover. The Area Managers, our new title, would move to a different office but the staff would stay where they were. I was moved to the South Office while M. P. was moved to my East Office. She took over a high producing and hard working group, while I took over her not so high producing and not so hard working group. The result was that in less than one year, the group that I had become Area Manager of rose to the top as rehabilitation providers, while my old office fell behind.

During all this time, Mary had principally raised the two boys. Alan had finished High school and two years at San Antonio College in Home building, had worked for Ray

Ellison Homes, and then later married Carrie Williams, had one child, Jessica, and joined the Army.

Mark finished High School, and went to San Antonio College for about a year, then went to International Bible College for about a year, then went to International Bible College where he finished his degree in Theology.

This allowed Mary and I to travel together quite a bit. She would go with me on the visits to the offices I supervised in Del Rio and Eagle Pass since these were overnight trips. We also went to the Conventions of TRC in Dallas, Houston, Corpus Christi, etc. We also went to the National Convention in Washington D.C., and then again to Washington D.C. for a special project I was supervising at San Antonio College. We were also involved in meetings of the San Antonio Area Rehabilitation Assoc., and the Texas Rehabilitation Assoc., where we would go to meetings and conventions, etc. These were fun times.

It was during this time that Alan had joined the Army, and we took the opportunity to travel to visit him and Carrie in Georgia. Being from South Texas, they missed Mexican food very much. Mary and I bought a couple dozen tamales, froze them, and when we left to visit them, we put them in an ice package and took them with us on the plane. Needless to say, they were a welcome gift. We enjoyed the visit there. A couple of years later, we were fortunate to visit them in

Maryland. Alan had completed almost three years of school in Communications, focusing on Satellite Communication at Ft. Mead. They lived in housing on base, and there were several apartments in a circle, with a fairly large open space in the center of the housing.

Two events happened there that are firmly stuck in my mind. One was the playing of "midnight croquet". This was accomplished by tying florescent tubes on the wickets so that you could aim for the proper shot.

The second was a crab boil. They bought, seems like a barrel of crabs, brought them to the circle, boiled them and everybody over ate. This was where Tony, our grandson, showed his daredevil side. The steps leading down to the ground from the apartment were pretty steep. Tony was riding a Big Wheel Tricycle, and not just on the ground, but from the front door to the ground down the steps. A very bumpy ride, but he made it. Also, Alan would tantalize all the neighbors by setting up his grill outside, putting mesquite wood in the pan, and cook steaks, etc., and have the wonderful fragrance travel throughout the complex. Nothing smells more appetizing than mesquite wood smoke and cooking steak or chicken, or whatever. We really enjoyed some side trips. We drove to Gettysburg Battlefield National Park and saw the battle field where so many young men died, from both sides of the War. It was a solemn occasion, made more so because one of our ancestors died here, Hockaday Brister. He was in the 13th Mississippi Regiment. On our way back, we stopped in Mt. Airy, Virginia and bought some super, fantastic peaches, called Windblow. Another great trip was to an Amish town, Intercourse Pennsylvania. We ate lunch in an Amish eating place. It was located in the middle of a large cornfield, and the food was served family style. It was good, but they felt we weren't eating enough. They just kept bringing bowls and platters of food. We finally waved the white flag and paid our bill, which wasn't too high. We drove back to Fort Meade in Baltimore and nursed our full tummies. On the way back, we followed an Amish buggy pulled by a horse, and I was happy to see that the handicapped were taken care of in Pa., on the back of the buggy was strapped a wheelchair. Since my job was in Rehabilitation, I was really interested. Our next fun trip was taking the Skyline Drive over the Appalachian Mountains. It was very beautiful drive and relaxing. Time passed, and we had to come back home, but we took some great memories with us. After Alan was discharged, he landed a job with a large banking group in Rixleyville Va. The group transferred monies between banks worldwide. They lived in a large house next to a large wooded area that was very nice. Shortly thereafter, Alan received a call from USAA to come to work for them. They sent him a plane ticket to come to San Antonio, and paid for the moving van to bring their furnishings here. He must have been good because he has been with USAA for many years and will retire in a year or two.

My experiences with the Medical and Vocational Rehabilitation earned a write up in the National Distinguished Service Registry of Medical and Vocational Rehabilitation.

——— Chapter Six ———

Retirement and Ranch Experiences

I retired from TRC in September, 1993 after 26 great years of seeing handicapped people go to work.

Mary and I spent a lot of time at the ranch, clearing land, building fences and buildings, raising and selling cattle, hauling hay, burning thorns off the cactus for the cows to eat. In between, traveling to Colorado, New Mexico, Utah, Arizona, etc. We bought a slide in camper for our pickup, which was self-contained with beds, icebox, stove, water with a sink, but no bathroom. We made several trips to Colorado because we couldn't spend a lot of time away from home, but we did see the Grand Canyon, and other attractions. We spent some nights in a camp ground where they had showers, etc. but many nights were spent where ever we found a place to pull off. Mary's brothers, Merle and Morris traveled with us in their own camper rig. The advantage of traveling as we did was to allow us to visit some places that would not be available in a car or on a tour bus. We did a lot in the 20 years that we were able to travel and enjoy "freedom".

When Mary's Dad passed away, the Ranch, 470 acres, was divided into four parts. The ranch was divided by IH 35, 390 acres on the South side and 80 acres on the North side. Mary asked for the 80 acres because it would be easier to divide between the two boys, Alan and Mark. Grace, Merle and Morris each had 130 acres, but the pieces were narrow, and long, roughly 650 feet wide, and over 5,000 feet long. After several years, the plan was altered because Merle and Morris sold their parts to a man who wanted to build a mobile home park on the land he owned next to Merle and Morris. Morris kept about 30 acres to protect the area of the ranch house. They all agreed that Grace and Morris would leave their property to Alan, and Merle would leave the money he received for his land, along with the 80 acres from Mary, to Mark. Enough! Mary and I started our ranching experience quickly. There were no buildings, no water lines, no stock water tanks, just land. In order to keep the Agriculture Exemption from property taxes, we had to purchase some cattle. We knew a man who went to cattle auctions and we asked him to buy us some stock. The first bunch he bought was a cow, two young heifers, and one small bull. The bull was short and stocky, so we named him Samson. The two small heifers started growing horns, so we called the Veterinarian to remove the horns. That was the bloodiest mess ever. We vowed we would not ever dehorn cattle again. Before buying the cattle, we needed a barn. We decided the barn would be 20 feet wide and 30 feet long, and would slope from fifteen feet in the front to twelve feet in the back. We went shopping for the material. We bought nine large creosote posts about eighteen feet long as we would dig the holes for them three feet deep and set them ten feet apart. We bought 2"X6"X 10' boards to put around the top of the posts to nail, the 2"X4" X 10' boards for the roof. The roof and sides of the barn would be corrugated metal. We finally bought all the materials we would need, including nails and long lag screws to fasten the boards to the posts. The next step was to rent an auger to dig the post holes. We got the holes dug and posts set, and then started putting the boards around the top of the posts. Since all the poles were the same height, we sawed off the surplus as we fastened the boards to form the top rafter which provided the required slope of the roof. With no electricity, we had to bore the holes with a brace and bit. Strictly manual labor. We started at the back and got all the side boards and back boards fastened in place. The work moved to the front, which was so tall that I had to stand on the step next to the top of the ladder. I drilled the holes and fastened the boards with no problems until we came to the last post that had to be drilled. I was drilling the last hole, and having to push hard against the brace to get the bit going into the wood. Merle was holding the ladder to keep it from tipping over and I was nearly through drilling when Merle became distracted and let go of the ladder. The ladder fell and so did I. l landed on my back and was stunned. Mary went to call an ambulance, (this was before cell phones were available) while the rest were doing something. To be honest, I wasn't aware of anything going on. The para medics said I had no apparent broken bones, and left.

We quit work for the day. After I sat up a little while, my side began to hurt. We decided I was not in any condition to drive home so Merle said we should go to the ranch house and spend the night there. By the time Mary had driven around to the other side of IH 35, I was really was really hurting. Bouncing along the dirt road to the house didn't make things any better. We finally arrived. Mary and Merle fixed a bit of supper, of which I didn't eat very much. As time passed and I was still hurting, Merle got up and said he couldn't stand to see me in so much pain. He went to the cabinet, got a large glass, and poured it full of Jim Beam whiskey. He gave it to me and I drank the whole thing, at least six ounces. Shortly thereafter Mary and I went to the ranch house to go to bed. (Merle and Morris were living in a mobile home next to the house). I undressed and crawled into bed. The whiskey kicked in and I didn't feel a thing all night. The rest did me some good because I didn't hurt as much the next morning. After eating a little breakfast, Mary drove us to town and straight to our Doctor. He sent me down for x-rays. After the doctor in the x-ray department looked at the films, he ordered a wheel chair and sent me back to my doctor with the films. I couldn't imagine why the wheel chair, but after my doctor told me that I had a compression fracture of the Thoracic spine between the 11th and 12th vertebrae, I understood the precautions. I had a cracked rib, but it wasn't broken, which was the source of my pain. I recovered, and two days later, we went back to working on the barn. I stayed off the ladder though. Eventually we finished the barn, and over the next several weeks, we built two more small sheds. We had to haul water from the ranch house side to our side for the cattle since we had no water supply handy.

Through a Federal Grant, the Atascosa Rural Water Supply Corporation was formed and the residents and farms were able to get a permanent water supply through the corporation. The only requirement was to purchase a water meter, which we did at a very low cost. The only problem is they located the meter at the back of the property, which meant we would have to lay a lot of pipe to get water to the barn at the front of the property. Initially, we decided to put a water tank closer to the water meter which was not a big problem. We only had to lay about thirty feet of water pipe. We dug a trench, attached the pipe to the meter, and then put a float valve on the tank to control the flow of water. This worked quite well for a few months, but it was inconvenient for the stock. Mary and I planned to put another tank at the top of the hill, near the middle of the property, a distance of about 1,000 feet. I pulled out my trusty shovel and started digging a trench about eighteen inches deep. The ground was soft except for one place that was rocky and I had to break the rock with a sledge hammer. We completed the trench and enlisted the help of Mary's brothers, Merle and Morris, to lay the pipe. The plastic pipe came in lengths of twenty feet so we had to buy the pipe and couplers, and the purple preparation liquid and the glue. With Mark, our son, added to the crew, we were able to lay he pipe fairly quickly. We left the trench open overnight so the joints could "cure". The next day we put another tank at the chosen location, installed the float valve and turned the water on. We walked the length of the pipe to be sure there were no leaks, and while the tank was filling I began to fill in the trench to cover the pipe. Success at last. The whole project took about two and one- half days. We were still determined to have water at the front of the place. But we waited a couple of years. The time came to lay pipe to the barn and sheds. This time, a little more thought was given to the project and we rented a ditch digging machine. I let Mark and one of his buddies do the trenching since they were younger and stronger. Mark was about twenty-five years old. I had to cut the pipe to the first water tank and install a "T" joint and a cut-off valve so that the water could be diverted to the West cross fence and then to the South to the barn. This was about two thousand feet of pipe we had to lay. I ordered the pipe, joints and glue and preparation liquid. After giving Mark a real head start on trenching, Mary and I began to lay pipe. She applied the prep and glue and I pushed the Joint onto the pipe, the process was repeated on the other end of the pipe and I would push the pipe into the joint. Eventually all the trench was dug and the pipe was put in place. The next morning we walked the pipe line to be sure there were no leaks and then began to cover the pipe. At last the work was done and we had water at the front of the property. The fences around the property were in bad shape. We were forced into fence building, but first we had to clear the brush and cactus away from the fences so that we could work.

Due to the necessity of having the pickup handy for tools and wire, we cleared about twenty feet of space from the fence. This took place in the summer, and it was hot. I would chop brush, saw the larger bushes, and Mary would pull the brush to the side, away from the fence and driving space. To give an idea of the magnitude of the clearing work, the front fence is 2,600 feet long, the West fence is 1,800 feet long, the back fence is 2,200 feet long, and the East fence is only 1,200 feet long. The only tool used that was not completely manual was the chain saw. After clearing the brush away, we had to take down the old fence, remove old wooden posts, roll up the old wire, dig holes for new wood posts, drive in the new steel posts, roll out the new barbed wire, stretch it and attach it to the posts, then we rolled out stock wire that is five feet high and attach it to the posts over the barbed wire. The barbed wire could be stretched with the "come-a-long", but I had to use the bumper of the pickup to stretch the stock wire. Not being super human, this process, clearing, removing old fence, building new fence took a few weeks. Mary and I were both in our early Sixties, so we took a little longer. We followed the old fence lines since we thought they were accurate. The man who owned the property next to our West fence had the fence surveyed and found that there was as slight bow in the fence which was taking in some of his property. He said we could buy the tiny part of an acre for $2,000.00. which would be cheaper than taking down the old fence and rebuilding it. We had our own surveyor come out and he marked the fence line for us with stakes. The fence only had to be moved to the East about two feet at the Widest part of the bow. We went to work and moved the fence, had our surveyor check it for us, then called his surveyor and had him confirm the accuracy of the fence. Everything was approved and we were happy.

After all the putting in water lines, building fences, clearing brush and building sheds and corrals, we were able to enjoy our life as ranchers. All we had to do was general maintenance, haul and unload hay, load cattle to take to the stock yard where they were sold, take care of any cuts, scratches, pink eye, and other things that can happen to cattle. We were not, by any means, large ranchers, but we had as much to do as did the large ranches, and they had a lot more help.

I want to share with you one of the reasons that we had to rebuild our fences. Our first bull was named Samson. He was a good bull and provided us with over eighty calves during his tenure. One day Samson did not come to the barn when we honked the pickup horn as he usually did. We went looking for him and saw that he was in the pasture next door. The man who was leasing the place did not have a bull so Samson, being a good neighbor, decided he would visit the cows next door and help things along. I searched and found the place where Samson went through the fence. I thought I would be smart and fix the hole he went through, and open a nice big hole away from the brush so he could get back home easier. I walked to where Samson was and started him back to our property. He walked along very quietly, heading for the hole he had made in the fence. I turned him to go to the nice big gap I had made for him and he walked along the fence to the gap, then right by it, as if it did not exist, then headed back across the pasture. I went after him again, he headed toward the original hole, walked by it again. Mary thought if she stood by the gap she might get him to turn in. He didn't. Back across the pasture he went. By this time, I was ready to rope him with a 30-30 rifle. However, cooler heads prevailed and we decided that if I closed the new gap and opened the old one, he might go into our pasture. I go back, chased Samson out of the brush around a dirt water hole, and prayed to God that He would help me get Samson home. God answered my prayers because Samson headed straight for the old gap, went through like it was an open gate, and ambled on toward the barn. I fixed the hole and we prepared to go home. To put this in perspective, it was in July, very hot with no shade, and lasted about three hours. Just one more "fun" thing that goes with handling cattle. Cattle will go back to the place they went through, so don't second guess them, like I did.

One of the disadvantages of having property on the IH 35, was people "dropping" their dogs that they no longer wanted. The poor animals would wander onto our property and adopt us. We couldn't let them go hungry so we brought dog food out each day and fed them. The first dog dropped was a Chow mix, very pretty and smart, and we named her Rusty. She protected the property and was friendly with the livestock. Unfortunately, after a few weeks, she tangled with a wild pig and was injured so badly that she died before we could get her to a vet. Sometime later, we arrived at the ranch to find another stray dog, a short hair mix, that was a pretty yellow color so Mary named her Buttercup. About two days later when we got to the ranch, we were met by a black Labrador stray dog. After watching him with Buttercup, and the way he walked, Mary thought Duke would be a good name. Duke and Buttercup were a good pair, got along very well, and as we became attached to them, we thought it would be better for them if we took them to the other side where Mary's brother, Morris could look after them. I had the stock trailer hooked on the pickup, so we put the dogs in the trailer and they enjoyed the ride to the ranch house. We left later that day to come back home and the dogs seemed content. The next day we went out and were met at the gate by the two dogs. We loaded them in the pickup- after we finished our work, and took them back to the house. Next morning, there they were again. We took them back the third time. The next morning, only Duke was at our gate. When we took him back, we found the reason he was alone. Buttercup had given birth to seven puppies. I bought some cable, and harness to tether Duke to a tree so he would not go back to our side. When we went down to the house the next day, Duke was miserable. We decided that the best thing would be to put him in the old chicken pen, with Buttercup, and keep him there. When we got to the ranch the next day, two things had happened. Duke met us at our gate, and after finishing our work, we took him back to the house side, and put Duke back in the pen. We looked for the pups and found one missing. I heard a faint noise and whining, but didn't see the source. I had stacked some hay bales in the shed, and when I got closer to the hay, the noise was louder. There was no sign of the puppy, so I moved some of the hay bales and found the puppy had climbed to the top of the bales and then fallen all the way down and was wedged between the bales and the side of the shed. I did not want to move all the hay, so I went to the back of the shed, located the puppy and pulled the tin siding out far enough to get the puppy out and return him to Buttercup. Then I arranged the hay bales so that such a mishap wouldn't happen again. We left Duke and Buttercup in the pen and went home. Guess who met us at our gate the next day. Duke had gotten out of the pen and crossed IH 35 to get to our side. When we went to the house, we took Duke, and I inspected the pen to see how he had gotten out. He had dug a hole under the fence and crawled out. I filled in the hole, put some rocks on the dirt, and hoped for the best. That wasn't good enough. Duke had gotten out again. This time, he had scaled a wooden pallet that had been placed close to the fence. I moved the pallet, and decided to "dog proof" the pen. I put heavy pieces of mesquite logs all around the fence to keep him from digging out, moved anything that was close to the fence he might climb, and thought we had Duke penned for good. No, duke met us on our side again. Back to the house to see what he had done. He had managed to move one of the heavy logs enough to be able to dig a hole. I decided I would place the deterrents on the outside of the fence so he couldn't move them away from the fence. I put heavy wood pallets with large rocks on them, and more heavy logs, thinking I had him penned for good. Nope, Duke met us on our side the next day. Not having a barrier inside, he had dug a hole and managed to move the outside pallet close enough to chew off part of the board and then crawl out. I guess Duke was "Super Dog" since nothing could keep him in the pen. He paid for his stubbornness, because what we feared would happen did happen. Duke was hit and killed while crossing IH 35. Buttercup was okay in the pen and happy raising her pups. When her pups were weaned, we knew we couldn't keep them, so we got permission to use the parking lot of Jupe Feed Store, and put up a sign "Free Puppies". In about thirty minutes we had given away all of them. Sadly a few weeks later, Buttercup suffered the same fate as Duke. That was the last of our doggie adventures.

Chapter Seven

Short Stories - Fiction

B.T. And Girlfriend

The Cush Maker

Doctor Highbinder

Faith Humor

Follow My Instructions

The Great Chupacabra Hunt

Ivan The Not So Terrible

Joke Time

The Lost Cowboys

Mr. Chan

Owl Man

Rockaferrous Wrens

Truck Driver

True Story

B.T. And Girlfriend

One day last year, 2014, Mary was feeling pretty good, so we went outside in the back yard to have a glass of tea and enjoy the weather. Temperature was around 90+ degrees. We noticed some unusual activity in the yard next door, and turned our attention to see what was going on. B.T. was out and really strutting his stuff, trying to get his lady friend's attention. (B.T. is the initials for the Boat Tailed Grackle). He flexed his muscles, pranced around, huffed and puffed, bent low to the ground, uttered some weird sounds, then really started to strut around. While all this was going on, the lady friend seemed to totally ignore him. The temperature was rising a little more, and B.T.'s temperature also seemed to be rising. After a few more minutes B.T. finally decided that he would give up. He turned away and headed for the nearest water, jumped in and took a quick bath. Mary and I decided he had reached a decision that it was too darned hot to try any more, and that he would rather be cool. It was really fun to watch.

The Cush Maker

Back in the time when the Armed Forces were trying to build their strength, following WWl, A young man was urged to join one of the service branches. He went to the Army recruiter and said he would like to join. The recruiter asked if he had any special skills he could bring to the Army. The young man said he was a Cush Maker. The Recruiter, not wanting to appear ignorant, said unfortunately there was no place for a Cush Maker in the Army. The young man went to the Marines and the events happened as they had with the Army. Next he went to the Air Force, same thing again. He was getting discouraged, but thought he would try the Navy, since the Navy took almost anybody. The Navy recruiter said they just happened to have an opening for a Cush Maker, so he was signed on and sent for basic training. Following 6 weeks of Basic training, he was assigned to a ship and they sailed out into the Atlantic Ocean. Several days went by and the Captain being anxious to know what a Cush Maker does, called the young man into his quarters and said that it had been almost two weeks, and that he wanted the young man to do his specialty. He responded that he was eager to get started. The Captain asked him what equipment needed. "I need a large steel ball with a handle welded to the top, I need a crane strong enough to lift the ball, and I need a large furnace". The Captain had his orderly order the items and have them placed on the forward deck. Soon all the equipment was in place so the young man went to work. He fired up the furnace and after it was burning good, he climbed on the crane, hooked the steel ball, lifted it onto the furnace, and waited for it to get red hot. The Captain was watching closely and really wondered if the sailor had a secret weapon. Finally, the ball was hot enough and the sailor moved the crane over it, hooked the ball, lifted it from the furnace and moved it over the side of the ship. When it was in place, the sailor dropped the ball into the water and as it hit, it made a large sound, CUSSSH. Another successful job.

Dr. Highbinder

Dr. High Binder, Anthropologist, loved to explore old ruins so when he discovered there was some very ancient ruins in South America, he jumped at the chance to visit them. He had a map showing the location in Bolivia, so he took off for Bolivia. He hired a guide and put together an outfit, and they started off into the jungle. They were making good progress, and in two days they were nearing the ancient ruins. Dr. High Binder heard a very strange sound. He asked the guide what it was, and he said it was a Foo bird, found only in Bolivia, and was actually pretty rare. The good Dr. wanted to see the bird, so the guide led him toward the place where the sound came from. The guide told him to be as quiet as possible so as not to disturb the bird. The good Dr., walking almost on tip toe, approached the tree where the bird was until he was right under the limb where the bird was sitting. Suddenly, the Dr. felt something hit his shoulder, and looked to see what it was. It was a big blob of bird shit. The Dr. was upset and started to wipe it off, and the guide shouted at him to leave it alone. The Dr. wasn't about to "let it alone", so he began to wipe the mess away. Suddenly, the Dr. was attacked by the bird. It was pecking him, and beating him with its wings. The Dr. was calling for help, and the guide came running over and helped him drive the bird away. The Dr. said, "what made the bird attack me?" The guide told him, you didn't listen when I told you not to wipe off the bird shit. All I can tell you now, since you know better, is "when the Foo shits, wear it".

Faith Humor

Three good friends got together to go fishing. They were a Catholic Priest, a Jewish Rabbi, and a Protestant preacher. They rowed out to a good spot in the lake and tossed out their lines. The fishing was pretty good and they were catching some large bass. The Rabbi got up and said that he had to go ashore for something, and when he was asked why he wanted to take the boat in when the fishing was so good, he replied that he would walk in. Well, he got out of the boat and started walking to shore.

After a time, the Preacher stood up and said he was going to go to shore also to take care of "business". The Priest was surprised to see that the Preacher also walked calmly to shore. The Priest was really concerned, as he recalled the time when Jesus walked on water to get to land, and he said, if those two could walk on water, then I, with my strong faith, can do the same. He stood up, stepped outside the boat, and promptly sank under water. He struggled up, and called out to his friends to help him. They turned around and walked back to help him. After they got him back in the boat they asked him, "What is the matter Father, don't you know where the rocks are? Moral: Faith is strong, and much needed, but a little knowledge will often smooth the way. Amen?

Follow My Instructions

Many of us have knowledge of people who are misers. This story is about one old miser who was going to prove that you can take it with you.

Mr. Miser had worked hard and made a lot of money in his lifetime. He was very frugal with his money and had accumulated quite a large sum. His wife never lacked for the bare necessities such as food clothing and shelter, she did, however, lack some of the little luxuries of life. She never complained about this to her husband, just accepted the situation and "made do" with what she had. One day her husband became ill and was taken to the hospital. After some time had passed, the doctor came out and told her that her husband was very ill, and probably would not live much longer. She went into the room where her husband was, and began to talk. He, being practical, wanted to discuss his funeral preparations. He told his wife he wanted a plain coffin, nothing fancy, and no flowers, or any of the usual trappings. The last thing they discussed was his fortune. He told her he wanted his money put in his coffin, and made her swear that she would. Being a dutiful wife, she said she would. She told her close friend about his request, order, to put his savings in his coffin. Her friend thought that was terrible and that she shouldn't do it. The response was that she had promised him and she would keep her word. A few days later her husband passed away, and she followed his instructions to have a plain coffin, and a quick service. After the funeral was over, and her husband had been lowered into the grave, her friend approached her and asked her if she had actually put the old man's fortune in the coffin as he had ordered. She said yes, she had followed his instructions. Her friend gasped and asked her how she had managed to get all that in the coffin without being seen, and have someone take it out. She responded that it was perfectly safe. She said "I wrote him a check".

The Great Chupacabra Hunt

Recently a local rancher by the name of Fritz found one of his calves dead, but didn't see much blood. Upon closer inspection, he noticed that the stomach had been ripped open and the liver was missing. Being well versed in the stories of the Chupacabra, he immediately knew that it was responsible for the death of his calf because the liver and blood were the parts that were preferred by it. Because the Chupacabra could cause considerable damage to his herd, the rancher called his neighbors and enlisted their help to build a trap and catch the beast and finally show the world that Chupacabras did exist. Now the rancher and his neighbors knew they did exist, but many people believed they were a myth and were always making comments about the people who knew they existed. Chupacabras are large dog like creatures with long fangs and really cause ranchers problems because they kill sheep, goats, and small calves.

The rancher gathered the boards and wire and other materials to build the trap. They wanted it to be strong, and have a heavy drop door to make sure it couldn't get out after it was caught.

The guys planned to be at the trap the next evening so that the trap could be baited with blood and liver. They all were to have flashlights and their rifles just in case. They showed up as scheduled and they had their ATVs also. Fritz baited the trap and they broke up into two groups. Fritz and Jim in one group and Tom and Jerry in the second group. The plan was for each group to go separate ways away from the trap and if they heard the Chupacabra they would radio the other group and they would converge so that they could herd the beast toward the trap. One thing was very apparent, they were noisy and lights were flickering all around like fireflies. Anyway, off they go, and as Fritz and Jim reached their location, they heard the strange sound made by the Chupacabra. They radioed the second group and told them that the Chupacabra was between them, and that they should drive toward each other and this would cause the Chupacabra to get close to the trap and smell the bait and enter the trap and it would be caught. After a few minutes, Jim hollered that he had seen the beast and that it was heading toward the trap. Being the cautious hunters, they cranked up the ATV and roared away toward the trap, being as quiet as a herd of longhorns in a stampede, with lights waving around, a real serious bunch of men. As they got closer, they heard the thud of the door dropping, and the long howl of the Chupacabra. They really went crazy, congratulating each other and it was only by a miracle that they didn't shoot off their guns. As they approached the trap, they heard the Chupacabra howling again. They ran to the trap door and peeked in but couldn't see very clearly what it looked like. While they were standing around talking, and planning how they were going to show off their catch, Tom looked down and noticed a footprint on the ground, but the foot print was about three times the size of Tom's foot. They said, that looks like Big Foot tracks. Jim said that he had heard that someone had seen Big Foot recently. Suddenly they heard a loud noise at the back of the trap, like boards being ripped off the trap wall. They cocked their rifles and started to the back of the trap, but as they reached the back, they saw a huge figure, followed by a smaller wolf like animal, fading into the mesquite trees. Big Foot, they shouted in unison, he was in the area as had been reported. The puzzling part was that the animal with him had to be the Chupacabra. After cussing and discussing the situation, they concluded that Big Foot had trained the Chupacabra to hunt and they shared the meat. Also, they agreed the howling done by the Chupacabra was to call Big Foot to rescue it.

Ivan The Not So Terrible

There once was a bear cub named Ivan, after the Russian Czar, Ivan the Terrible. He was a small Grizzly bear, about three feet tall when he stood on his back legs. He felt proud of himself because he considered himself a real mean bear. He wasn't too good about staying home because he liked to prowl around different parts of the forest. One day he told himself that he had explored all the territory around home, and it was time to go further into the woods. His mother bear would not allow him to go too far from her sight, but one day she became distracted and Ivan saw his chance and took off for the big adventure. He was not afraid of being hurt because he was a "big" Grizzly and other denizens of the forest had just better watch out. His mother had been telling him that he had better talk with papa Grizzly before going off on his own or he could be in big trouble. Ivan did not care because he could take care of himself. Papa wasn't around so Ivan disappeared into the forest. He had a great time, chasing rabbits, squirrels, birds and anything he could find. He was really feeling good about himself so he went a little deeper into the forest. Meanwhile, his papa came home and was told that Ivan had gone into the forest by himself, so papa went looking for him. Ivan was happily exploring things, unaware that a huge mountain lion had smelled his scent and was on his trail. After some time had passed, the lion spotted Ivan a little way in front of him. The lion crouched down and started creeping up on Ivan. Something caused Ivan to look around and he saw the lion. Ivan, in his most mean Grizzly fashion, stood up on his back legs, raised his front legs and let out a mighty roar! At least he thought it was mighty, but more like a squeaky shout. To his surprise, the lion crouched down, acted nervous, and then turned around and headed for the forest as fast as he could run. Oh, what a swelled chest Ivan had. He had actually chased off the lion. I don't know how bears strut, but Ivan was doing some posturing. He turned around to see if any of the animals had witnessed his great feat. To his great surprise, he saw his papa bear behind him. Papa bear stood about 8 feet tall, and had a mouth that could have easily swallowed the lion's head. Ivan then realized that he hadn't scared the lion, but it was his papa who actually had scared the lion. Ivan was really glad to see his Papa, and that his Papa had seen him stand up to the lion. He had convinced himself that he could not be hurt, but then realized that he was only as bad and mean as the one who had his back. Suddenly the reality of the situation hit him and he was thankful that Papa had found him. We should always hope someone has our back in similar situations.

Joke Time

A man was just admitted to the State pen. That night his cell partner called out loud, number 25. There was a sudden multiple laughs from the cell block. Then someone else called 34, again there was a big laugh. Another one called 62, this went on for quite some time. Finally the new guy asked his cell mate what was going on. The response was, we have been here so long that we told all the jokes we knew, and it finally got to be a burden to tell the same joke over and over, so we gave each joke a number so that when we wanted to tell a joke, we would just call out the number. The new guy said, let me call a number. The cell mate said o.k., so the guy called out 42. There was no sound. He called 42 again, still no sound of laughter. He asked his cell mate what was wrong? His reply, "it is all about how you tell the joke". LOL

The Lost Cowboys

Back in The Texas Panhandle, Cowboys were often faced with finding cattle on the range and get them to safe places when one of the famous Texas Blue Northers with snow blew in. Cattle will turn their backs to the wind and try to get away from the wind by moving in front of the wind. Such was the situation on the Double Dot ranch one Winter evening. The hands had just finished eating Supper and were looking forward to a nice warm bunkhouse. The Foreman came in and told the boys to saddle up and go get the herd that had been spotted on the grass about a mile from the ranch house earlier. He said that a Norther with snow was heading their way, and they had to move the cattle or they would be pushed over some cliffs by the river. It isn't hard to imagine the things the cowboys were saying as they put on their heavy coats, went to the barn and saddled their horses. Most comments were aimed at the cattle that didn't have enough brains to stay in one place. Anyway, being good riders, they took off and soon were with the herd. They started them moving toward a canyon that was sheltered from the wind, and would provide some relief from the pending snow. After they got them settled, they started back to the ranch house. They had only gone a little way when the storm hit with all its fury. They tied their hats on with their neckerchiefs, turned up their coat collars and hunkered down for the cold ride home. In a few minutes the snow was blowing so hard and it was so dark that they lost all sense of direction. They rode for quite some time, and finally agreed that it was too dark and too much snow to know where they were, and they better stop or they might get lost and wander around and get frost bite or maybe even die. They got off their horses and gathered some grass and "buffalo chips", another name for dried cow patties, to build a fire. They huddle around their intended fire and nobody had any matches. They were really in trouble. Cold, snowy, and no means to start their fire. Suddenly one of the hands said that he had read somewhere that if you took a bullet, pried out the lead, and put the gunpowder on the fire material, and then fired the pistol, the muzzle blast would set the powder on fire and you would have a fire. He was roundly congratulated for saving their lives. So, a bullet was produced, the lead pried out, the powder poured on the fire materials, and all was ready. Our hero, pulled his gun, aimed it at the fire stuff, pulled the trigger and, folks, it is hard to visualize what happened, so I will tell you. The shot did not set off the powder, instead it blew everything away, and the most dreadful thing was that the shot scared the horses and they all took off. Now the situation had turned deadly, no fire and no fire material, their horses were gone, along with their bedrolls and blankets, and they were stranded somewhere on the ranch. They finally decided to curl up on the ground and not expose too much of their bodies to the cold and snow. A little before daybreak, they woke up and were waiting for the sun to come up so they could get their directions. In a little while, they heard some noise and when they were able to see very far, they saw a building. As it became lighter, they saw it was their ranch house, and the cook was preparing breakfast. They said at least they were saved, but they didn't know what happened to their horses. So, with chagrined looks on their faces, they headed toward the ranch house. They thought they would stop in the barn first and make it look like they were coming from there before going into the house to have breakfast. When they looked in the barn, there were their horses, contently eating hay. That was the final straw, they walked around, cussed at everything, and threatened to hang the cowboy who had ruined their fire.

The only thing that stopped them was how could they explain to the foreman that they had spent the night in the cold and snow, when they were only about a hundred yards from the bunkhouse and their nice warm beds. They thought the best thing to do was keep quiet and pretend that they were in the bunkhouse all along. Life on the range.

Mr. Chan

Mr. Chan, a Chinese furniture maker was noted for his skill in building shelves and cabinets, tables, etc. He used various kinds of wood, but preferred teak because of its color and texture. One morning he went out to his shop and noticed that his supply of teak had almost disappeared. He was sure that he had plenty when he went home the night before. He began to look around to see if he could find out who had taken his teak. He saw some bare foot prints that looked like a young boy. He was puzzled as to what a young boy would want with his teak, and thought about the young boys in the neighborhood who could have any use of the wood, but wasn't able to think of anyone. He wasn't happy that he had to go to the lumber yard and purchase more teak because of the extra cost of the wood and the loss of time to meet his obligations as he had some shelves to make. That evening, he looked at his supply of teak, and noted that he had enough for tomorrow's work. Home he went, had supper, and after a bit of rest, went to bed. The next morning, he had breakfast and went to his shop. The first thing he noticed he was missing teak, and the same small bare foot prints. He was very irritated that he had to go to the lumber yard again, but he did and laid in another supply of teak. He determined that he would find out who was taking his wood, so after he finished his work for the day, and had eaten supper, he returned to his shop to stand guard. About two hours later, he heard a noise, and looked out to see a bear taking his wood. He ran out to stop the bear, and noticed that its foot prints were those of a young boy. He ran after the bear, shouting, "stop, boy foot bear with teak of Chan". The bear dropped the wood and ran into the forest. Although he was frustrated he hadn't caught the bear, he was happy that he had saved his wood.

Owl Man

In the heart of the Appalachian Mountains lives a legendary creature know as Owl Man. He has been described, by those lucky enough to see him, as at least six feet tall, weighs about 190 pounds, has large wings, and terrible red glowing eyes. The main reason he was named Owl Man was the fact that he is a carnivore and hunts small animals. Except for the large eyes, wings, and eating habits, he doesn't resemble an owl at all. He does not kill, or eat humans or large animals, but does hunt smaller animals. He is said to have powers not related to any other living being. He is supposedly able to "teleport" himself from one place to another in an instant. One witness said that he saw him standing in one place, and when he called to his buddies to look, the creature had instantly moved to another location. He also was able to go straight up into the air. Also, it is said that if you stare into his eyes, you could go into a hypnotic state, or become ill. Some witnesses said they became very nauseated and had terrible cramps in their stomach. Because he was so strange looking, and people didn't know anything about him, many stories and superstitions were circulated about him. One day, a group of guys got together and began to discuss Owl Man. After having several shots of moonshine, they began to talk about catching Owl Man and killing him. Why kill him? One drunk said because he is so danged different, and not one of God's creatures, but from the Devil. They all nodded their heads and agreed that only the Devil could make such a thing. They began to make their plans. One of them was still pretty sober, so he got their attention and said. "Look, he is called Owl Man, and what attracts owls?" One said "a female owl". "No, you idiot" said another, "Food is what will attract this owl. The others nodded their heads and agreed that food was the thing to draw Owl Man. Next came the discussion as to how they could trap the Owl Man after getting him close to the trap. The bright one of the bunch said first we have to devise a trap. We need to have a trap that would hold the creature, and figure a way to kill it. Shooting it won't work because he can transport himself so fast that we couldn't get a shot before he disappeared. One of the guys said "alright Mr. Smarty, what do you plan to use as a trap"? "Mr. Smarty said it is very simple". He is called Owl Man, and owls are drawn to food. We need a plan to kill him after he reaches the trap." Suddenly, Mr. Smarty said boys, you know what a bug zapper is don't you? Of course, they said, the bugs fly into the lighted cage and are zapped by electricity. But where do we get a cage big enough to hold him, and the electricity to zap him? "Are you all so dense that you can't think?" said Mr. Smarty "We make the trap out of stock wire and hook it up to my generator which will provide the electricity, and Zap, we have him".

The group broke into cheers at the revelation of making "the world's largest bug zapper", although they didn't expect to zap any bugs. This caused one member to question why they were building a bug zapper to catch Owl Man. Mr. Smarty, patiently explained to him that when Owl Man hit the electric fence, he couldn't teleport away like he had done before and would be killed there. They eagerly began to make plans for the trap, and how to get the Owl Man to the trap. One member said he had some leftover fence that he would provide, another said he would get the rabbit to put in the trap to attract Owl Man, Mr. Smarty has the generator, now all we need is a place to put the zapper. "This old bridge is perfect" said Mr. Smarty," the metal may help intensify the electric shock". Everyone went to get the things needed and soon all gathered at the bridge eager to implement their plan. They rolled the wire into a large circular shape, wired it together, and placed it on the bridge girder. The generator was put in position and terminals were hooked to the wire cage. Soon all preparations were finished and they only had to wait for dark for the fun to begin. One of the guys, very safety conscious, reminded the men not to look directly into the red eyes of the Owl Man, because they could be hypnotized, or have a fainting spell, or some other reaction, and to remember that just because they may see the creature in one place, it could appear somewhere else in an instant. Also, stay away from the bridge after the generator started, or they could be zapped. At last it became dark enough for them to start their plan for capture. They moved away from the bridge into the woods. One of the group was told to start the generator and put the rabbit in the trap to attract the Owl Man. In a few minutes they heard the sound of flapping wings, and an odd vocal noise very close. They heard Owl Man pass over them and go toward the trap. After they waited a few minutes, they started toward the trap. When they got closer to the trap, they heard the "zapping" sound of the trap. They began to cheer and tell how they were going to be such heroes, and bring fame and fortune to the area. They all rushed to the trap and as they turned on their flashlights they were very excited to see what they had trapped, and then shocked at what they found. It was a great horned owl. This was their Owl Man. They were embarrassed, although they had gotten an owl, they had not been successful in getting Owl Man and after all their talk about how famous they would be. They swore a pact that none of them would tell what they caught, only that they had not seen or heard anything resembling the Owl Man. They also agreed that they would try to downplay the Owl Man, and vowed they would not attempt another such adventure. Now Owl Man is safe.

Rockaferrous Wrens

This is a story about some rare birds. Many years ago, there were a group of birds who lived in holes that they dug out of soft cliff sides. They liked these holes because they were located away from predators, and allowed them to fly in and out of their nests easily. As time passed, and the bird population grew rapidly, there was no longer enough space for the younger birds to nest. The younger birds were forced to relocate, but unfortunately, there were no soft cliffs available since they had become rock like in the passing years. What to do? One of the smarter birds said, I know of a place where iron ore is located. With iron, we can line our beaks and be able to penetrate the hard crust of the cliff to drill our nests, and It isn't too far from our location here in the Big Bend Country. It's called Iron Mountain, in Llano County, and we can fly there and back in one day. So a large delegation set off to Iron Mountain, where they found the iron ore, and began to form "iron" beaks. They flew back to Big Bend and proceeded to show how the iron beaks would work. Some of them started hammering at the cliff side, and after about a minute, they stopped. Asked why they stopped pecking, they said they had one terrific headache. It seems that the pounding of their beaks caused too much vibration on their heads, and cause the headaches. What to do now? They had the means to drill the holes, but the headaches were too painful to stay at the work long enough to do much good. Suddenly, one of the brighter birds said, "I know, let's go to the Chihuahua Desert, where they have these plants that provide a sap that is like rubber". Terrific idea, so off went the iron beaks to look for the rubber sap.

When they got there, they obtained the sap, and coated their beaks where they joined their heads. After they applied a good padding of rubber, they flew back to the cliffs, and began to pound away. They were able to complete the nest holes without any headaches, and the iron protected their beaks. Shortly thereafter, the flock was able to move into their new homes. More time passes, and birdwatchers of long ago decided that this was a new species of bird, and after observing how they made their nests, they agreed that this species would be named "Rockaferrous Wrens". So, when you travel around the Country and come across cliffs where there are numerous small holes, you will have found a colony of the famous Rockaferrous wrens.

Truck Driver

A truck driver was hauling a load of cars for a small car dealer in a sort of rural town, not close to a big town which is why he had a dealership. Anyway, the trucker had been on the road for almost a week and was anxious to get home. He looked at his map and found that he could take a County road and cut off about 45 minutes of his trip. It was getting late, about 10:00 p.m., but he wanted to get the load there and then he could get home the next day. He was tooling along, happy to be near the end of his trip, when his headlights went out. He stopped, found out a fuse had blown, but he also found he didn't have a replacement.

After turning the air blue with his unhappy remarks, he was resigned to spend the rest of the night in his truck as he couldn't see the road. He started to get in his truck and happened to look up at his load of cars, and not being as dumb as he thought he was, he realized that he could turn the lights on the top car he was hauling, and use those lights to see the road. Very happily, he climbed up and turned on the headlights, got in his truck, and started merrily along his way. About thirty minutes later, he saw a car coming toward him. The car slowed down, then suddenly swerved off the road into a ditch. The trucker stopped to see what had happened, and to make sure the driver was o.k. When he reached the car, the driver got out. He was o.k., but sort of nervous. The trucker asked him why he had suddenly swerved off the road. The guy said "when I saw how high those headlights were, I got off the road as fast as I could because I thought if that thing was that tall, how wide would it be", and I didn't want to take any chances.

True Story

Not a groaner, but a true story. A professional gambler was having heart problems. He went to a Cardiologist who diagnosed him as having a "leaky" valve between the Left Auricle and Ventricle. He told the gambler that he would have to replace the valve, or he would possibly die from heart failure. The gambler agreed, and he was scheduled for surgery, the valve replaced, and he went home after recovery, doing very well. After he returned to his profession, he found that he was losing continually, and this was not his usual way of playing. He finally figured out the problem, and promptly sued the Surgeon and the heart valve manufacturer. The valve was constructed such that the top of the valve was like an inverted basket, and a ball inside the basket acted as a normal valve, opening and closing according to the beat of the heart. After a few weeks of losing continually, he discovered that he couldn't win because the other players knew when he had a good hand, or a bad hand and tried to bluff. When he had a good hand, his heart beat would increase, and the ball in his artificial valve would click as it went up and down. The better his hand, the faster his "clicking" would be. Since this ruined his profession, he couldn't earn a living, so he sued for loss of ability to support himself and his family. I don't know, maybe this is a groaner after all! The valves did click though.

APPENDIX

Copy of Letter Announcing My Birth

Hello Grandpas, Grandmas, Aunts and Uncles,

Just a line to let you know that I have just arrived, as hale and hearty 91/2 pound boy that you ever saw. I am somewhat mad at this time, will be better later. My hair is black. I would love to see you soon. Lovingly, Alvis B. Brister, Jr.

Dad continues. P.S., he came unexpectedly at 12:36 a.m. February 15, 1934. Flora got along just fine, compared to previous times. She wondered if you would still come about Sunday. Well, Flora and "he" are both asleep, and we are thinking of taking napping. La Vona said to tell Grandma she could sleep with her.

Well good night,
Alvis B.

Vogt Family Tree

The following is a very brief summary of the Vogt (Voigt) family from the time of immigration to the United States from Prussia, now known as Austria, and settling in New Braunfels, Texas. From the book, History of New Braunfels and Comal County, Texas, from 1844 to 1946, I have obtained the following information.

Wilhelm August Ferdinand Voigt was born in 1822 in Birkholz, Dramburg, Hinterpommern, son of Gottfried Adam Voigt and Dorthea Sophie Borke. He married Johanna Ebert, born in 1846 in Schmaltentin, Pommern, Prussia. They migrated to Texas aboard the Johann Dehardt ship which landed at Indianola about 1846.

Wilhelm and Johanna Voigt arrived in New Braunfels after landing at Indianola on the Gulf of Mexico, circa 1846, and whose name appears, with that of his wife and children, in the 1860 census of New Braunfels, page 290. Wilhelm and wife, Johanna arrived in Texas in the late 1840s since Wilhelmine Voigt was born in 1850. The listing is:

Wilhelm Voigt, age 38, from Prussia (born 1822)
Johanna Ebert Voigt, age 36, from Prussia (born 1824)
Wilhelmine Voigt, age 10, born in Texas (born 1850)
*Johann Gottlieb Voigt age 7, born in Texas (born 1852)
Wilhelm Voigt(Jr.), 5, born in Texas (born 1854)

As near as can be determined, Wilhelmine Voigt, married a man named Loep and was known as Mina.

Johann Gottlieb Voigt married Frances Koletz, and their children were:
*Anton John Vogt, born Dec. 2, 1897, died November 4, 1962
G.H. (Henry) Vogt, born unknown
Frances Vogt, born, unknown
Agnes Vogt(Clara)?, born, unknown

*Anton John Vogt, Born December 2, 1897, died Nov. 4, 1962. Married Linnie Madge nee Williams Vogt, Born January 29, 1892, died July 15, 1973, around 1918. Their Children were:
Merle Vogt, born November 7, 1920, Died June 6, 2002. Never married.
Morris Leroy Vogt born November 12, 1925, died November 7, 2004. Never married

Grace Lillian Vogt, born September 27, 1930. Married Edmund Brysch, 1971. No children, died March 10, 2013.

Mary Frances Vogt, born March 2, 1935, Married Alvis B. Brister, Jr., June 3, 1955. Children are:

Alan Brian Brister, born March 26, 1957, married Carrie Lynn Williams, June 20, 1982. Children:

Jessica Rene, born June 1, 1984, San Antonio, Texas. Married Matthew Thibodeaux, March 29, 2008, Child, Alexis Violet, born April 15, 2009.

Anthony Brian, born March 11, 1987, Groveton, Georgia

Mark Timothy Brister, born May 8, 1967, married Vivian Mohn, born August 17, 1963, on August 15, 1992: Children are:

Esther Mary, born January 30, 1998

Mark Timothy II, born September 9, 2000

Ezekiel Caleb, born October 24, 2003

It is to be noted that before the 1850 census in New Braunfels, the Voigt name was changed to Vogt, either through misspelling, or through a desire to make the name easier to spell, or from some governmental official. At any rate, the name on the titles of land and the birth certificate of Anton John Vogt, father of Merle Vogt, Morris Vogt, Grace L. Vogt, and Mary F. Vogt were changed from Voigt to Vogt.

When I Gave A Bride Away

By

Al Brister

Mary and I only had two boys, so what I am about to tell you is one of the good things that happened to me while I was a Counselor with the Texas Rehabilitation Commission.

Not many men can give a "daughter" away in marriage when they have no daughter of their own. I did, and I was fortunate to be able to do it. The wedding took place in 1971, just before I was promoted to Supervisor in 1972.

I had a client named Blanca who had been diagnosed with Myasthenia Gravis, a condition that greatly limited her in the kind of work she could do. She was just out of High School, and was very smart. After I accepted her as a client, did some diagnostic workup, and assessed her capabilities, TRC provided the funding for her to be enrolled in San Antonio College in the Medical Assisting Course. She really liked the course and was making good grades. While there she met a young man, and they wanted to get married. While they were making plans, Blanca came to me and asked if I would "give her away" since her father had passed away, and she was living with her Uncle, but she didn't want him to be the one who would give her away. She told me that I had been so helpful and had given her good advice and talked with her when she was having a problem, and I seemed more of a father to her than a Counselor, and she wanted me to be part of her wedding. I was totally taken aback at this, and honored to be asked. I agreed, and she told me they were having a rehearsal in two days. She was Catholic, and the ceremony involved a lot more than I had experienced in my wedding, or other weddings I had attended. The rituals performed were fairly elaborate and beautiful. We had a successful rehearsal, and I awaited the big day. I suddenly learned why my father and Mary's father were nervous at our wedding. The wedding day arrived, and we all gathered at the church. Blanca was beautiful in her wedding dress, and the Groom was very handsome. I have pictures she gave me of us walking down the aisle toward her husband to be. We looked rather good I think, but it was great to see her and him together. I was relieved when the ceremony was concluded. After she completed the course work at San Antonio College, she came in one day said they were moving to California where her husband was hired into a good job in Los Angeles. A couple of months later,

I received a letter from Blanca that she had been accepted into UCLA to continue her education in the Medical Field. She really whizzed through her college work and finally she completed her Master's Degree. I don't recall the Major, but I think it had to do with Hospital Administration. I haven't heard from her in many years, so I don't know if she stayed in California or moved to some other place.

Printed in the United States
By Bookmasters